PUFFIN BOOKS

FIVE THINGS
THEY NEVER
TOLD ME

Rebecca Westcott was born in Chester. She went to Exeter University to train as a teacher and has had a variety of teaching jobs that have taken her to some very interesting places, including a Category C male prison. Rebecca now teaches in a primary school and lives in Dorset with her husband and three children. Her acclaimed first novel *Dandelion Clocks* was published in 2014, shortly followed by *Violet Ink*. *Five Things They Never Told Me* is her third book.

Visit Rebecca at www.rebeccawestcottwriter.com and follow her on Twitter @westcottwriter

FIVE THINGS THEY NEVER TOLD ME

REBECCA WESTCOTT

PUFFIN

PUFFIN BOOKS

UK | USA | Canada | Ireland | Australia
India | New Zealand | South Africa

Puffin Books is part of the Penguin Random House group of companies
whose addresses can be found at global.penguinrandomhouse.com.

puffinbooks.com

First published 2015
001

Set in Sabon LT Std 12.5/16.5 pt
Typeset by Jouve (UK), Milton Keynes
Printed in Great Britain by Clays Ltd, St Ives plc

A CIP catalogue record for this book is available from the British Library

ISBN: 978-0-141-35864-2

www.greenpenguin.co.uk

MIX
Paper from
responsible sources
FSC® C018179

Penguin Random House is committed to a
sustainable future for our business, our readers
and our planet. This book is made from Forest
Stewardship Council® certified paper.

*For my fabulous little sister, Elizabeth.
The idea for this book came from a story she
told me and she didn't even moan a little bit
when I abruptly ended our phone conversation
so that I could start writing! Thank you,
Lizzy – your support and love and sisterly
brilliance is never taken for granted.*

*And for Pauline and Brian, my granny and
granpa, who shared their own memories
and experiences and stories with me.
I love you both very much.*

CONTENTS

FAMILY GROUP*

Having a choice is not always a good thing. Sure, choice is great when it comes to menus and films and clothes and books. I like choosing when it's a choice of ice-cream flavours (mint choc chip, every time) and I like choosing what music to listen to on my iPod. I do not like choosing between my parents, though, which is what they asked me to do exactly forty-one days ago.

* *Family Group* (1948–49) by Henry Moore. This sculpture is supposed to show a family the way it's meant to be. You know, a kid and a couple of parents, all close and hugging each other. Yeah, well, I reckon that someone needs to make a new sculpture, because not all families look like this. My Family Group would show a screaming mum walking away, while the dad sat quietly with his head in his hands and the kid plugged herself into her iPod and wished that they'd all just shut up. That'd be way more realistic.

'We're not asking you to choose between us,' said Dad.

'Absolutely not,' agreed Mum, although her eyes told a different story.

'We just want you to make the right choice for YOU, Erin. We can't make this decision for you. You're old enough to decide for yourself.'

That made me mad. Every single time I've asked if I can do something exciting they've told me that I'm too young; that they are the adults and they know what's best for me. All of sudden, just because it suits them, I'm old enough to make my own decision.

So I did make my own choice. Dad thinks I chose him because I must love him more. Mum thinks I didn't choose her because I mustn't love her as much. A week later she packed her bags in silence and gave me a hug and told me that I could change my mind any time. She said there would always be a place for me in the huge house she now lives in, along with a tall, sad-looking man called Mark who has found his reason to live again now that he's stolen my mum. Him and his tragic little boys who have taken my mum to fill the gap left in their home by his dead wife. I hope they'll all be very happy together.

But the truth is that I chose neither of them. Not that they have any idea. How could I possibly choose between two people who didn't choose ME? After all the fighting and yelling and sobbed conversations about betrayal and waste of a marriage, after the arguments about who was going to keep the TV and the teapot that had been a wedding present and the chair that Mum said was a family heirloom from her grandmother but Dad said that he always sat on, after all that, they were remarkably calm about who got to keep me. There was no shouting about that at all. It's like nobody actually wanted me. I am less important than a teapot.

No – I didn't choose Mum OR Dad. I chose Picasso. If it wasn't for him I don't think I could have survived the last few months in our house. Every time it got bad I would head to my room where he would be waiting for me. He's not supposed to be in my room but there's no point in following the family rules when we're not actually a family any more.

So now Mum's gone and it's really fine. Dad's out at work every day and when I get home from school the house is empty. It feels a bit weird sometimes but I tell myself that another word for silent is *peaceful* – and it's definitely better than the suffocating atmosphere that I would feel when I stepped through the door and into the middle of another one of their rows.

And it's not like I'm actually alone. As I close the front door and turn round I can hear him leaping out of his basket and bounding across the kitchen floor. I crouch on the floor and laugh as he runs up to me, his slobbery face pushing against mine as he says hello. Picasso might not be able to talk but he can tell me exactly how he's feeling without words, which is a good thing because I've had enough of words to last me a lifetime.

I go into the kitchen and tip the contents of my school bag on to the table. Most of my homework can wait until another night but I'm quite keen to make a start on my art project. Miss Jenson has given us our summer holiday homework early because she says that it's such a big project we might as well get going on it right away. I love art. I suppose I must have got that from Dad but we never really talk about it .We never really talk about anything, actually.

I pull my art book towards me and turn to a fresh page. Our project is called 'What Art Means

To Me'. Everyone groaned when Miss Jenson told us about it but I think it sounds kind of fun. We have to choose different pieces of artwork and write about how it makes us feel. What it makes us think about. There's no limit to the number of pieces of art we can choose but the more we do the better our grade will be. To get us started, Miss Jenson has given us all a picture of a sculpture by Henry Moore. It's called *Family Group*, which right away puts me in a bad mood.

Dad's late home tonight and I've written my reaction to Henry's sculpture and put some sausages and chips in the oven when he walks into the kitchen. He looks tired, which is pretty much how he always looks at the moment.

'How was your day?' he asks me, putting his workbag down in the corner and then turning the kettle on.

'There's no water in there,' I tell him as the kettle starts to whine in protest. He picks it up and walks across to the sink and I wonder what he would do if I wasn't here.

'Was school OK?' he says but I can tell he's not really desperate for an answer. He's making sure that he's done the Dad-routine. It's been Thirty-four Days Without Mum and he's pretty much asked these questions every day. *Have I asked Erin about her day?* Check. *Have I made sure she's eaten some food?* Check. *Has she got money for lunch tomorrow?* Check. He thinks he can relax if he's done all of this – that he's fulfilling his duties as a father. I think he's doing the best he can but it doesn't come even close to being good enough.

The smell of burning drifts through the kitchen and Dad scowls.

'Have you put something in the oven?' he asks me, rushing across the room and opening the oven door. Smoke pours out and he steps back, flapping the air in front of him and grabbing the oven glove.

'Erin! What have I told you about this? You're twelve years old, for goodness' sake. Far too young to be using the oven when I'm not here. You could have burned the house down!'

He pulls out the tray and we both look at the charred remains of the chips. They look disgusting.

Dad sighs. 'I can't believe you've done this AGAIN. I have to be able to trust you, Erin. What were you thinking?'

I look at the floor, trying to keep my anger hidden.

'I was hungry,' I whisper, my voice shaking with fury.

'There's no need to cry,' Dad says hurriedly. He can't stand me showing emotions of any kind, particularly not anything he thinks is girly. He just has no clue about how to deal with it. 'Don't feel bad. We all make mistakes.'

He thinks I feel guilty. He thinks I'm looking and sounding like this because I know I've done something wrong. I can feel the blood rushing through my veins, getting ready for me to explode at him. I try to swallow the nasty taste in my mouth but it's no good. It has to come out. I look up at Dad and let him have it.

'I DON'T feel bad!' I say. 'I was HUNGRY! It's six o'clock and I've been at school all day and I needed to eat some food. You weren't here! And I thought I was supposed to be old enough to make my own decisions now?'

Dad looks surprised for a moment and then he glares at me.

'I wasn't here because I was working. Which is how I get the money to put this food on the table. And I don't appreciate you ruining decent food and then having the nerve to shout at me. There's a family rule, Erin –'

I snort when he says this but the look he gives me stops me from saying anything else.

'There is a FAMILY rule that you do not use the oven when you're in the house on your own. And until you hear otherwise, that is a rule that you will follow. Understood?'

I glare back at him and for a second we are standing in silence with sparks of rage shooting from our eyes. 'UNDERSTOOD?' he repeats and I know that I'm going to have to lose this one.

'Yes,' I mutter, looking away. Let him have his family rules if it makes him feel better. Personally I think he's completely deluded if he thinks we're a family. How can two people who can hardly bear to be in the same room as each other count as a family?

'I'm just trying to keep you safe,' he says, dumping the chips in the bin and rescuing the sausages from the oven.

Whatever. Keep telling yourself that, Dad. We both know it's got nothing to do with that and everything to do with Mum leaving and you being stuck with me.

Dad gets the bread out of the cupboard and puts it on the table with some butter. I get some plates and we sit, silently making sausage sandwiches, which I am too furious to eat. Dad tries to start a conversation but I'm not interested so in the end he gives up and turns on the television. I know that he won't let me go to my room until I've eaten my tea so I try to eat as fast as possible, but the bread sticks to the roof of my mouth and the burned sausages taste like misery and each mouthful needs me to chew it about a million times before I can manage to swallow it down. And with each swallow I plan how to show my dad that I am a force to be reckoned with. That I can't be shoved in a corner and just forgotten about.

THE SCREAM*

It takes until Saturday morning, Thirty-seven Days Without Mum, for me to get the opportunity I need. I probably wouldn't even be bothering but Mum rang last night and Dad insisted that I talk to her, despite the fact that I was obviously gesturing to him to tell her that I was out. I had to stand in the hall, holding the phone away from my ear, while meaningless words floated out of the receiver as she went on and on about how

* *The Scream* (1893) by Edvard Munch. This freaky painting shows a figure in front of a red sky. Nobody knows why he's screaming but I think it's obvious. He's sick and tired of nobody listening to him, that's why. He knows that just normal talking isn't going to get him noticed, so he screams instead. And it works, because everyone in the world knows this painting. His scream got him some attention.

much she's missing me. She started saying how she wished that tomorrow were one of 'our' Saturdays – like that's suddenly a thing, and how she's still my mum. Words are easy to say – if she really meant it then she'd still live in the same house as us. Anyway, Dad caught me not listening and had a real go at me afterwards. So he's brought this on himself. He's still in bed and I've checked that he's fast asleep by listening at his bedroom door – I can hear faint snores coming from the other side so I know it's safe to carry out my plan.

I get dressed quickly and creep downstairs into the kitchen. Picasso trots over to me and bumps my hand while I fill his bowl with dog food. Once he's distracted and munching away I tiptoe towards Dad's workbag, which is lying in the corner of the room where he always puts it when he gets home. I know it's silly but I really don't want Picasso to see me doing this.

I kneel down and open the zip. Inside the bag is Dad's skanky lunchbox that he hasn't unpacked yet and some of his tools. I take all of this out and rummage around in the bottom, my heart pounding until my hand closes on the thing I'm looking for. Pulling it out I open up his wallet.

Staring up at me is a photo of me, Mum and Dad, taken on holiday last year when we were still the three of us. I don't know why he's kept that in there. Ignoring the happy, smiling faces I open up the cash compartment and remove eight £20 notes. That's a start but it won't get me very far – not with the day I've got planned. Rooting through the old receipts I strike lucky.

'Yes!' I hiss, holding up Dad's debit card. This is exactly what I need. I stuff the wallet back in his bag and then shove the tools and lunchbox on top, zipping it back up. No point in alerting him earlier than necessary. Turning round I see that Picasso has finished eating and is staring at me across the room, his head on one side and his eyes looking mournful. Picasso is a black and tan dachshund with one brown eye and one blue eye. One half of his face is white and the other half is dappled brown and black. He's the weirdest-looking dog I've ever seen. Mum says that he suits me – that we're both highly interesting and unusual. Except that I can't be *that* interesting, or she wouldn't have wanted to replace me.

Anyway, Picasso looks like his face has been split down the middle. That's how he got his name. I've always loved those weird paintings that Pablo Picasso did of faces, all wonky and multicoloured, plus the artist Picasso had a dachshund called Lump who he really loved. I've got a copy of the picture he drew of Lump, on the wall in my room. It's just one line but it really does look like my dog.

'It's OK,' I tell him. 'I'm just borrowing it really.' I feel bad saying this but I really don't want Picasso to think I'm dishonest. He pads over to me and I sit down next to him, burying my head in his soft, furry coat. I suppose I could always put the money back? Dad would never know. I could just pretend this hadn't happened and make him a cup of tea and then let him cook me bacon and eggs for breakfast and take me out for a picnic and a walk at the sculpture trail, like he said last night. Dad's got a piece that's being displayed as part of the trail and he's been promising for ages that we could go and take a look.

But then I remember how I felt when he was mad at me about the burned chips. And I think about how he says he wants me to act my age and grow up but never actually lets me do anything fun. I think about how he still takes Mum's side, even though she's not here. And I remind myself that I'm just an inconvenience to him. That neither him or Mum wanted me and I'm just a problem that needed to be solved.

And who wants to waste a beautiful Saturday morning on a rubbish walk, looking at a load of carved wood, anyway? Especially when it's mostly the reason that Mum left in the first place. It used to drive her crazy that Dad had got this amazing talent but that he 'refused to do anything with it'. That was what she said. She used to go on and on about how, if only he'd believe in himself, he could sell his sculptures for thousands of pounds and then he wouldn't have to work as a badly paid gardener at a care home. Then he'd tell her that he *liked* being a gardener and that the day he started creating his sculptures for money and not for love would be the day that he stopped making anything worth looking at. I've got no idea if she even knows that he's got a piece being shown in the sculpture trail. I suppose it's a bit late now, anyway.

I rub my hand one more time down Picasso's firm back and then I stand up. They think I'm a problem so I'm going to show them that they're right. That should make them happy – maybe they'll finally find something they both actually agree on.

The bus driver starts to make a fuss about me paying for my fare with a £20 note but I just look at him and tell him it's all I have. He mutters about how he's not going to have any change for the rest of the day, but I smile sweetly and he gives me a ticket, grumbling under his breath. I go straight to the back of the bus and look out of the window as we drive towards town. I've done this before lots of times with Lauren and Nat but it's the first time I've been on my own. Everything looks a bit different today. Brighter and sharper and a little bit scarier. Maybe that's because I know that there's no way I can wriggle out of what I'm about to do. There's no way I can say it was an accident, that I didn't mean to do it – because I am doing this one hundred per cent on purpose.

We reach the town centre faster than I thought we would. I get off the bus and look around me. Where should I go first? My stomach starts rumbling and I remember that I haven't had any breakfast yet. I'm right next to the coffee shop where I have to meet Mum every other Saturday but I hate that place now and I know that Dad would go crazy if he thought I was getting breakfast in McDonald's so I head there and order food to take away. It's sunny today, only two weeks until the summer holidays, so I find a bench and sit outside watching the shops come to life while I eat my Egg McMuffin. It tastes surprisingly good – especially when I imagine what Dad would say about me eating junk food this early in the morning.

When I've demolished my breakfast I scrunch up the paper bag and lob it towards the bin. It goes in and I grin to myself.

'Nice shot!' says a voice behind and when I turn round I see a boy chaining his bike to a lamp post. I recognize him from the year above me at school, but I've never spoken to him before. I look behind me to see if he was talking to someone else but there's nobody there and when I turn back, he's smiling at me.

'Thanks,' I say.

'Good breakfast?' he asks, nodding in the direction of McDonald's.

'It was OK,' I tell him. I'm not usually shy but there is something about this boy that is making me feel self-conscious – possibly the fact that he's totally gorgeous. I wipe my mouth with the back of my hand, praying that I haven't got any remnants of egg on my face.

'See you then,' he says and saunters off down the road. As I watch him go I realize how much I want him to stay. I'd like to talk to him properly, not just mumble some rubbish about food. I want to yell at him to stop but I know I've got no reason to call him back.

I stand up and brush my hands off on my jeans. Today is already turning out to be more interesting than I thought it would be.

The cash starts to run out really quickly. It's amazing, really, how expensive everything is. I've only bought a few art supplies, some jeans and a couple of tops and I've spent £95 when I add in the bus fare and the McDonald's.

I have decided that the best way to show Dad how I'm feeling is to hit him where it really hurts. In the wallet. All he does is go on and on about money and how we have to tighten our belts because we've only got one wage coming in now. Well, whose fault is that? Not mine. Thirty-seven Days Without Mum and he's already told me that my pocket money is going to have to contribute towards my clothes and any school trips that come up. That's totally unfair. I didn't ask for any of this so I fully intend to stock up on everything I'm going to need before he starts deducting my funds. I'm very aware that after this, I probably won't get any more pocket money until I'm eighty-five, but at least I'll have bought all the essentials. And I'll have shown him that he shouldn't EVER boss me about.

But now I've spent some of the cash I'm going to have to carry out the second part of my plan. I must admit, I am nervous about this part. It seems a little bit worse than just taking money out of his wallet. OK, quite a lot worse. But I know that this is the only way to get what I want – and as him and Mum have done what they want without any consideration about me, then I think it's OK for me to behave like this, just for one day.

I walk towards the cash point that I've seen Dad use and pull out his bank card. He uses the same code for everything, which is exactly what you're not supposed to do. It's like he's asking for trouble, really – he should know that he's just making himself an easy target. *Anyone* could steal his card and take his money. I look around me to check that nobody is watching and then I put the card in and key in the numbers of my birthday. It works! I press the button for taking money out and then look at the choices. £10? £20? £50? £100? I think about what I'm planning on buying and make a decision because apparently I am now old enough to do that. Pressing my finger on the screen I watch as the machine whirs and magically spews £300 out and into my hand. Then I fold it up and stuff it into my pocket, its bulk making me feel like a bank robber.

In the Technology Store I make my way straight to the stand where the iPads are displayed. I have been asking for one of these for months but Mum and Dad always say that it would be a waste of money for someone my age and I should count my lucky stars that I've got an iPod Shuffle. I've tried telling them that it'd help me with homework but they just won't listen – and now Mum isn't even around for me to ask any more. Her and Dad have an arrangement where I have to meet up with her every fortnight but she said it wouldn't be 'healthy' for her to come home and there's no way I'm going to Mark's house, so we have to meet in town. The coffee shop is not the best place to concentrate on Pythagoras' Theorem. An iPad would totally help me get better grades at school.

'Can I help you?'

The shop assistant is looking at me suspiciously like I'm going to shoplift or something. I feel offended – there's no *way* I'd ever take something that didn't belong to me.

'Yes,' I tell him. 'I'd like this, please. In black.'

He looks at me. 'It's great, that model, but you know it's really expensive, don't you?'

I make a huffing sound under my breath. 'Yes, I know. I have the money,' I say.

He pauses, looking straight at me again, then appears to make a decision. 'In that case, if you wait by the till I'll just go and get you one already boxed up.'

He walks towards the back of the shop and I go over to the till. The shop is busy and it's taking him some time to get back to me, so while I wait I look out of the window. Suddenly I see HIM again – gorgeous, scruffy-haired boy. I start to lift my hand, ready to wave, but then I see that he's talking to a girl and my arm drops back down to my side. I watch as they walk past, her all long legs and him laughing, and I feel a bit less happy than I did a moment ago.

'Here you are.' Snotty shop assistant is back and is smiling now that he's going to make a sale.

He places the box on the counter and I look at it longingly, hoping and hoping that Dad isn't going to make me take it back when he finds out what I've done. I take the bundle of notes out of my pocket and put them on the counter. Snotty man looks at me with one eyebrow raised.

'Birthday money,' I explain. 'I've been saving.'

'Ah,' he says. 'Well, it's a good choice. I've just got one of these and it's fantastic. Just make sure nobody steals it. I've got my name engraved on the back of mine – makes it less tempting to thieves!'

I look at the box and then I look at him, an idea starting to form in my mind.

'You can do that? Get it engraved with your name?'

'You can get it engraved with anything you like!' he laughs, friendly now.

'I want to do that!' I say. Dad can't make me return it if it's actually got my name on it, can he?

'Sorry,' says the shop assistant. 'You have to order online if you want it engraved. We don't do it in-store.'

That's not good. Getting my name engraved would have meant I could definitely keep the iPad forever. Otherwise there's a big risk that Dad might make me bring it back to the shop and get a refund.

The shop assistant must see how disappointed I am because he leans across the counter and smiles at me.

'You could always pop over to the jeweller's across the road,' he tells me. 'My friend did that and it didn't cost much. They did a good job too.'

I look out of the window to where he's pointing and see the jewellery shop that he's talking about.

'Thanks!' I say, picking up the carrier bag that now contains my most precious item in the whole, entire world. 'I'll do that.' Then I walk out of the shop and go straight across the road before my courage fails me. I can't even begin to imagine what Dad is going to say when I get home.

Fifty minutes later and I am sitting on the bus, heading back to goodness-knows-what. I am trying to remind myself that I deserved to have this day – that Dad brought this on himself – but the closer the bus gets to my stop the more nervous I start to get. Maybe I should have left Dad a note to let him know where I was. When I checked my phone earlier I had about a hundred missed calls from him. I sent him a text when I was waiting for my iPad to be engraved, telling him that I'd be home soon but I suppose he might have been a bit worried about me.

I get off the bus and walk slowly down our street. My carrier bags feel heavy in my arms and suddenly I feel like I'm holding a bomb. Perhaps I've been a bit over the top? I just wanted to let Dad know how mad he makes me feel – I wanted him to hear me for a change, not just tell me that this is how things are these days and expect me to put up with it. I want him to know that I have an opinion too. Plus I really, really wanted an iPad.

As I trudge down the front path I see a movement at the living-room window and a few seconds later the front door is flung open and Dad is standing there. And he does not look happy. He gestures for me to go inside and I walk past him and stand in the hall, wondering for the first time what he's actually going to do. And I'm wondering why I didn't stop to think about that before I took his money and bank card.

THE FOREST*

The last two weeks have been horrendous. I've been allowed out of the house to go to school or to help Dad with the supermarket shopping, but that's it. No hanging out in the park with Lauren and Nat, or going into town for a laugh. He drove me to the coffee shop to meet Mum last Saturday morning but that doesn't exactly count as going out. He wouldn't even let me go over to Nat's

---

* *The Forest* (1927) by Max Ernst. This picture makes me feel like it's hard to breathe properly. The trees are so close together and the spaces between them look like zips – as if at any moment the trees might get zipped together and the sky will be shut out. The bird is trapped in a cage, surrounded by scary, sinister forest and no matter how much it cries it can't get free. This picture means only bad things. It reminds me of the story of Hansel and Gretel – that story always gave me serious heebie-jeebies.

house to work on our science project, which meant that we looked really stupid when we did our presentation in class because we hadn't had a chance to practise. I thought I might be able to go to Lauren's when I was taking Picasso for his walk, but Dad's started coming with me. We stomp along in silence, as fast as Picasso's stubby little legs will go. It's grim.

When I got back from town that day, Dad made me sit down in the kitchen and 'explain myself'. There wasn't really much I could say. He looked in the carrier bags and went a bit pale when he saw what I'd bought in the Technology Store. Straight away he said that it had to be returned – and that's when I showed him what was engraved on the back.

Erin Edwards

I thought he'd start yelling at me and I braced myself, but he didn't say a word. He just looked at the words for what felt like an eternity and then he carefully put the iPad back in its box and sat in silence, looking at me from across the table and glaring.

I cracked after about two minutes.

'I never get anything I want!' I blurted at him. 'It's completely and utterly unfair!'

He looked at me for a bit longer and I could feel my face burning red under his gaze. I wanted him to scream and yell at me, to tell me how furious and angry he was with me. But he still didn't say a word.

I felt a tear trickle down my cheek and I desperately scrubbed it away. I thought that all I wanted at that moment was for Dad to say something – anything. But I was wrong because as awful as the silence was, the words, when they came, were much worse.

'I thought you'd gone to live with Mum,' Dad said eventually, his voice really quiet. 'I rang her and told her that I thought you'd changed your mind. That living with me was too difficult for you.'

I looked at him in astonishment. How could he ever think I'd leave Picasso?

'But Mum said you weren't there,' Dad continued, 'and then, just after you sent me that text, I saw that the cash and bank card from my wallet were missing. I made a picnic for our day out while I waited for you to come back. I thought that there must be a reasonable explanation. I thought I *knew* you, Erin.'

I looked round then and saw the picnic on the counter – packets of sandwiches neatly wrapped in greaseproof paper, the juice of the tomatoes leaking through in places. Cheese and tomato – my favourite. The sight of the sandwiches with a couple of apples stacked next to them made me want to cry.

'I wanted to trust you, Erin. But you've shown me that I can't and that makes me sadder than anything else that has happened over the last few months. We're a family, you and I, and we stick together. We don't steal from each other. HOW COULD YOU DO THIS TO ME?'

He shouted the last bit and I flinched. I don't think I've ever seen my dad that angry in my whole life.

He'd stopped talking then and looked away from me, as if he was trying to stop himself from saying something more. I wanted to say sorry but the word just wouldn't come out of my mouth and I started to cry instead.

'You obviously won't be keeping this,' Dad said to me, picking up the iPad box and standing up. 'And you've lost all your privileges. That means no pocket money and no spending time with your friends outside of school until further notice.' He told me that the clothes would all be going back to the shop but that I could keep the art supplies and I'd better make them last for a while because there would be no more coming my way for quite some time.

I didn't even bother to argue. I guess a part of me always knew that someone with my rubbish life would never be lucky enough to keep something as amazing as an iPad. And actually, I was feeling pretty awful about making Dad so worried – although he didn't have to yell at me like that.

So the last two weeks have been totally terrible. Dad barely spoke to me for the first week and I have been SO bored. This last week has been a bit better, though – I helped Dad wash the car after school on Tuesday and he actually talked to me like I was a normal human being. I think he's starting to forgive me. And I'm feeling pretty good today. It's the last day of school and I've spent the whole day making plans for the summer holidays with Lauren and Nat. I've got no money but I'm fairly sure that Dad will reinstate my pocket money from tomorrow – after all, he's not going to expect me to entertain myself for six weeks without any funds. I've taken my punishment and now we can move on – I can get my life back.

Mum keeps phoning me up, trying to get me to go and visit her new house. I tried saying that I didn't want to talk to her but Dad got really cross again so now it's just easier to hold the phone away from my ear while she rambles on. When we met in town last week she asked if I wanted to go on holiday with her and Mark and her two substitute children, but I politely declined. Actually, I said that I'd rather eat my own toenails for breakfast than spend two weeks in sunny Spain with them. She laughed, like she thought I was joking – but then she realized that I wasn't being funny and she stopped laughing and put on that false 'concerned-parent' voice that she uses with me these days and said that I was very welcome to go with them and that if I was going to change my mind then could I please do it soon while they could still get me a plane ticket. I just munched my blueberry muffin and ignored her.

Dad will be working at the care home all summer – apparently old people don't get a summer holiday off from being old and he'll be needed five days a week. He's the grounds manager, which means that he does everything that needs doing in the gardens and the house. He's always going on about being lucky to have a job and that there are always lots of interesting people around to chat to – but I can't think of anything worse than being stuck with a load of old people, blathering on about the 'good old days' to anyone who will listen.

So, I've got a summer of freedom ahead of me and it can't come soon enough. The last few months have been horrible. It's now Fifty Days Without Mum and I'm hoping that I can just have a nice, normal holiday, hanging out with my friends and chilling with Picasso.

The plans I've made today with Lauren and Nat have put me in a great mood and I'm whistling while I grate the cheese, ready for our tea. Dad must have actually listened to what I said the day that I burned the chips and since then he's tried to make sure that he's home a bit earlier and he always leaves me with jobs to do that will make sure we're not eating too late.

'You're in a good mood!'

I've been whistling so loudly that I didn't even hear Dad coming in. I turn and look at him, a big grin on my face. It feels a bit weird, the way my mouth wants to smile, not scowl – but I'm really happy today.

'It's the summer holidays!' I remind him, pouring myself a glass of juice. 'Do you want some?'

'That'd be lovely,' he says, putting his bag on the floor and then opening it and removing his wallet. He slips it into his back pocket and I turn away – I don't want my good mood being ruined with a reminder of how little he trusts me.

Dad sits down at the table and I join him.

'I was making plans with Lauren and Nat today,' I tell him as he downs his juice in one gulp. 'And I was just wondering if you might be thinking about starting up my pocket money again. I'm going to need some cash for bus fares and drinks and the cinema and stuff – nothing big.'

Dad puts down his glass and looks at me in surprise.

'You've been banned from going into town, Erin,' he says. 'You won't need any money over the holidays.'

I literally cannot believe my ears.

'You mean you're grounding me for the entire summer holidays?' I ask him, my voice sounding squeaky and indignant. 'You do know that's SIX whole weeks, don't you?'

'I am aware of the length of the summer holidays,' he says, his voice calm and flat.

'You're going to keep me prisoner in the house for six weeks, all on my own?' I can feel my heart racing in my chest. This is too harsh. I know I did a bad thing but surely I've paid the price over the last two weeks?

'You stole four hundred and sixty pounds from me, Erin,' Dad reminds me, as if he can read my mind. 'And no – I have no intention of "keeping you prisoner" as you so dramatically put it. You're going to have plenty of fresh air and lots of people to talk to. You might even grow up a bit.'

I do not like where this is going. I want to put my fingers in my ears and sing '*la la la*,' very loudly.

'I've agreed it with my boss and she says it's fine. She thinks the residents will love having you around for the summer. And I've spoken to your mum and she thinks it's a great idea.'

'I'm coming to work with you? To the old people's home?' I whisper, horrified.

'It's a care home, Erin. I'll be there to keep an eye on you. I think you could really get a lot out of it. There're some residents with amazing stories to tell – all they need is someone with the time to listen.'

I push my chair back and stand up, knocking the chair over in my hurry to leave the room.

'You have just officially ruined my summer,' I shout at Dad. 'I seriously hate you right now!'

'Well, learn to deal with that because this is happening,' says Dad. 'There's no way I can trust you on your own for the summer. Look at the damage you managed to cause in one morning.'

'But it's NOT FAIR!' I screech at him. Never in a million years did I think he'd go this far. 'What about my plans with Lauren and Nat? They'll stop being my friends if I don't see them for the whole summer!'

'I'm sure that's not true,' Dad says. He has absolutely no idea what he is talking about. Being part of a group of three is fantastic most of the time, but there's always a bit of a worry that the other two might be best friends with each other and I'm just the hanger-on. If Nat and Lauren spend the whole summer together without me then I'll be doomed to be the add-on friend FOREVER.

'And anyway,' he adds, 'you should have thought about that *before* you stole my money.'

'You can make me go but you can't make me talk to any of the oldies!' I scream at him, stamping towards the kitchen door. I don't care any more – there's nothing he can do to me that would be worse than this.

'No, I can't,' agrees Dad, sounding incredibly calm in the face of my raging anger. He probably feels really smug and proud of himself – he thinks he's found the perfect way to punish me and turn me into the sort of daughter that he really wants; the sort of daughter who will chat to old-age pensioners and make them cups of tea and learn to knit while all of her friends are having the summer of their lives.

I will not talk to one single person in that stupid place, I vow to myself as I stamp upstairs. *There is nothing that any lame old person could tell me that would be even a little bit interesting. They won't understand anything about my life – they were twelve about a million years ago. I bet they don't even remember anything except being old.*

MARTHA

There is nothing I hate more than old people. Constantly going on about their bad backs and their gammy hips and other medical problems that I have no desire to hear about. It never ceases to amaze me that the rest of society expects us to enjoy each other's company, based purely on the commonality of us all being over the age of seventy-five. Pensioners are no different to teenagers in that respect. Some old people are nice; some of us are foul. Some are good-natured and are happy to spend their days knitting and chatting while others of us are grouchy and angry and would rather stab ourselves in the foot with a knitting needle than suffer the indignities of attempting to *knit one, purl one*.

And no. You do not get a prize for working out which group I belong to.

I would like to say that I haven't always been bad-tempered and troublesome but it wouldn't be the truth. As a girl I was a constant source of worry and disappointment to my parents. I just didn't understand why there had to be so many rules. Rules about who I could be friends with; rules about what I could wear. Rules about what time I had to be home.

I found the last rule particularly difficult to abide by. I remember one evening having far too much fun to be home in time for my curfew. When I eventually returned my parents were furious. They said I wasn't allowed to see my friends for three whole weeks, which frankly I thought was a bit much. Not that it spoilt my fun. I would send a note to Tommy telling him to meet me outside our garden at certain times and then I'd pretend to be going to bed. As soon as the bedroom door was closed I was out of the window, climbing down the roof of the outhouse and into the back garden. I wasn't caught once.

It's just a shame that my climbing days are over. Life at Oak Hill would be a whole lot easier if I could sneak out of my window. At least I'd stand a fighting chance of that awful care worker not catching me in the act.

If you ask me, it's a total disgrace. I was born in 1929 and I believe I have enough years behind me to know what I want. And if, in my final months on this earth, I choose to smoke the occasional cigarette now and again then that is only my business. Oh, I'm not saying that smoking is a nice habit. I actually find it fairly unpleasant and there's nothing worse than the sight of yellowed fingers and foul teeth. And apparently, it does something quite disgusting to your insides.

No, it's not that I think smoking is a particularly good idea. I just don't like being told that I can't do it. It's the same with alcohol. In all honesty I'd prefer a nice cup of tea, but laying down ridiculous laws about what we can and cannot do just makes me cross. I'm too old to be told.

So apparently, I am now officially on *strike one*. I am 'upsetting the other residents' with my militant behaviour. They have suggested that I may be happier elsewhere. That made me laugh. As if happiness is a necessary emotion. Three strikes and Oak Hill will no longer be prepared to provide for my complex medical and behavioural needs.

Let the games commence.

LANDSCAPE FROM
A DREAM*

'Erin!' Dad is calling up the stairs and I wonder if I can get away with ignoring him. I wonder what he'd do if I burrowed down under my duvet like a little rabbit and refused to come out. Then I sigh and sit up. He's already mad with me – not that I care, but I know him when he's like this and the only chance I have of convincing him to let

* *Landscape from a Dream* (1936–38) by Paul Nash. I love this oil painting. There's a mirror that reflects a landscape totally different to the landscape in the painting. I think it means that things aren't always what they first seem. That maybe, if you turn round, you'll find something that you weren't expecting. It reminds me of a book that Mum gave me that had been hers when she was younger, called *Marianne Dreams* by Catherine Storr. Totally freaky but in a good way.

me stay at home is to go along with what he wants for a few days. Maybe if he thinks I've taken my punishment without too much fuss then he'll relent and let me have at least a few weeks hanging out with Lauren and Nat.

I get dressed in an old pair of shorts and a T-shirt and then grab my school bag and empty out all my schoolbooks and pencil case. I won't be needing *them* for a while. I fill my bag with the essentials needed for a long, boring day – my iPod Shuffle, a book, my sketchpad and a box of pencils. And then, even though it makes my bag super-heavy, I add a couple of Dad's art books that I took from the shelf in the living room. I'm getting quite into my art project so I may as well use the time to carry on with it while I'm hiding from old people. Then I trudge downstairs, deliberately stamping on each stair with a heavy foot so that Dad knows how miserable he is making me.

He meets me in the hall.

'Here you go. Drink this and I'll meet you in the car,' he says, handing me a glass of juice.

'What about my breakfast?' I am utterly aghast. I'd get better treatment if I were in prison.

'I called you to get up at least half an hour ago,' Dad tells me. 'If you'd wanted breakfast I assumed you'd get out of bed. You can eat a banana and a yoghurt on the way.'

I sink further into complete and total misery. The only motivation for getting out of bed these days is the thought of a hot piece of toast, slathered with strawberry jam and eaten sitting on the floor, with Picasso leaning against me. It's how I've eaten nearly all my breakfasts since she left, and as it's now Fifty-three Days Without Mum it has become quite a habit.

Dad pulls on his work boots and opens the front door.

'I need to get some tools from the garage – I'll expect to see you in the car in two minutes.'

He walks outside and I pull a face at the back of his head. But there's no point in standing here sulking. If I want breakfast I'm going to have to sort it fast, so I head into the kitchen and grab a banana. I ignore Dad's suggestion of yoghurt – I really would have thought he knew me better by now. Yoghurt has always tasted sour to me – it reminds me of sick and there's no way I'd *ever* eat it for breakfast.

There's just time to check that Dad's fed Picasso, give him a quick hug and tell him that he can get out through the dog-flap if he needs a wee. Then I put my bag on my shoulder and leave the comfort of my peaceful, quiet home. Old people and endless boring days, here I come.

My first impression of Oak Hill Care Home is not good. We go through a sinister pair of iron gates and turn down a drive. I want to ask Dad how he could possibly have brought me here, to this freaky, remote place. It's probably haunted. *This is my summer holiday!*, I want to shout at him, but then I remember that I'm not talking, as a protest that nobody ever listens to me, so I stay silent and look out of the window.

We drive through what feels like miles of dark, crowded trees and then we're suddenly here. Yeah, Oak Hill is a definite contender for housing things that go bump in the night. Dad parks the car and I get out, standing on the gravel and looking up at the huge house that seems to loom over me. Despite myself I am starting to feel a tiny bit excited. Maybe hanging out in a spine-tingling, ghost-infested mansion could be quite a cool thing to talk about when I go back to school in September.

We walk into the reception area and the spooky, Gothic vibe instantly disappears. Straight away I can tell I'm going to hate it here. It reminds me of school – everything seems fake. It doesn't feel like a proper home at all. Before Granny Edna died I used to visit her all the time with Mum and her house was crammed full of trinkets and knick-knacks. Stuff she'd collected over a lifetime that used to remind her of all the places she'd visited and all the things she'd done. I'd pick up some tacky little ornament and she'd go off on some long story about a holiday in Devon or a boy she once courted. I'd laugh when she said stuff like that and tell her that nobody says 'courted' these days – but, secretly, I quite liked hearing her stories and she'd always look so happy when she was remembering the old days.

I don't know how the old people who live here can ever remember anything, because it's all so bare and clean and impersonal. There can't be any memories for them here at all.

Dad walks me down a corridor and into a large, sunny room. It's filled with chairs and sofas. There's an old man sitting in front of the TV but I don't think he's watching it because his eyes are closed. I wonder for a minute if he's even alive, but then he twitches a bit and shuffles in the chair and I realize he's just sleeping.

'You can sit in here if you like,' says Dad. I look again at the old man and shake my head. He might die while I was sitting next to him. Or even worse, he might wake up and want to talk to me.

'OK.' Dad starts walking through the room towards a door on the other side and I scurry to catch up with him. 'Then you can help me out in the garden.'

This is not what I had planned, but it suddenly seems like the best of the rubbish options available to me. Dad shows me where I can stash my bag and then hands me a trowel. He doesn't seem in the slightest bit bothered that I haven't spoken a word to him since we got out of the car. I don't actually think he's noticed.

He leads me outside and round the corner of the house. I am not an outdoors kind of person but even I can see how beautiful these gardens are.

Dad points to a flower bed.

'This needs weeding,' he tells me.

I must look puzzled because he smiles at me and crouches down on the grass. 'You see all of these green bits? They need pulling out. Put them in a pile at the side and I'll be back to check up on you in a while.'

He ruffles my hair and strides off in the opposite direction to the way we came. I kneel down on the grass and look at the flower bed. Everything looks quite green to me. I have totally no idea which ones he said were the weeds.

I spend a few minutes pulling random bits of plant out of the soil and chucking them on the grass. This is so dull and even though it's still quite early I'm getting pretty hot. Dad will be really mad with me if I've been pulling up his prizewinning flowers instead of weeds, so probably the most sensible thing to do is stop before I get it completely wrong. Maybe I should scope out the rest of the gardens – get a feel for the place where I'm going to be spending the majority of my summer.

I stand up and rub the soil off my hands. My knees have got green grass-stains on them and I look like a little kid. The thought makes me angry and without bothering to search for Dad I stomp across the lawn and on to one of the gravel paths that lead away from the house.

As soon as I'm out of sight I feel myself starting to relax. I'm on a little pathway that twists and turns round bushes and under trees. The sunlight can't get through and the air feels different – full of something interesting, maybe. I keep walking, stepping from shadow to shadow and leaping over the occasional puddles of sun that have managed to slip through the heavy branches above me.

And then I'm out in the open. The brightness makes me blink and it takes me a few seconds to register what I'm seeing. And when I can see properly, my brain can barely make sense of it. Because what I'm looking at is utter perfection.

Hidden among the trees is a clearing. It's obviously still part of Oak Hill because I haven't gone over any fences or stiles, but it looks like it's a forgotten part of the garden. The path has stopped and there's a strip of grass stretching down to a stream that winds its way through the bottom of the clearing. On the other side of the stream is a steep field that reaches up to the horizon, making it feel a bit like a secret valley. Everything is wild and overgrown, filled with buttercups and weird, random plants that I haven't ever seen before. I take a few steps forward and when I turn round it's almost impossible to see the opening where the path begins – it's hidden from view and I can tell straight away that nobody can see me here.

A sudden feeling of excitement bubbles up inside me and I want to laugh out loud. My own secret hideaway! I can spend the summer here, doing what I want and nobody can make me listen or talk or do any stupid jobs. It's completely perfect. I want to whoop and run about for no reason, or lie down and roll around on the grass – and I haven't felt like doing those things since I was little. It's a shame I'm too old to do them now because this place is crying out for someone to play in it.

I walk around the top end of the clearing, peering through the undergrowth and making sure that I really can't be seen, that it really is as private as I think it is. Thick trees surround the grassy area and it's completely impossible to see anything on the other side. As I get towards the middle I can see that there is a bench, hidden under what even I can tell are weeds. Yanking at the long strands I try to free the bench from captivity but the plants have been there for a long time and I can't budge them. I need serious tools for this job and I know just the man to give them to me.

But there's plenty of time for that. For now I'm happy to sit on the grass, hugging my knees up to my chin, and looking down towards the stream. This place is mine.

THE WATERFALL *

It's been Sixty Days Without Mum. I saw her yesterday (a walk in the park this time, instead of our usual coffee shop) and all she wanted to talk about was whether I'd changed my mind about going on holiday with them. I could tell by her extra-smiley face that she was confident I'd give in, that I'd much prefer two weeks in Spain to going to Oak Hill every day with Dad.

'Mark's happy to pay for an extra ticket,' she told me. 'But time's running out, sweetheart.'

* *The Waterfall* (1943) by Arshile Gorky. When I look at this painting it feels like I can almost hear the sound of running water. I like abstract paintings (although sometimes I do think that maybe I could just chuck some paint on a canvas and give it a random title and sell it for millions). This painting looks peaceful to me.

I wanted to tell her that, on the contrary, time is growing, not running out. After all, I'm not counting down the days until I SEE her, am I? Every day is another day marked off on my calendar – the days without her are mounting up and if anything, time seems to be getting faster. It feels like it'll be no time at all before it's been Eighty Days Without Mum, and then Ninety-nine Days Without Mum and before I know it, it'll have been six months or a year and it'll be normal for everyone except me.

'I can't leave Picasso,' I told her, and then ignored her while she went on and on about how Dad can look after him and how she misses me and really wants to spend some 'quality time' with me. I couldn't help thinking that if she wanted to see me that much then she should have fought to keep me with her. Then she bought me a mint choc-chip ice cream as a treat so I told her that I only eat vanilla now – that mint choc chip was totally yesterday's flavour. She looked kind of surprised and a little bit sad too but I'm not going to let myself feel bad about that. It's not my fault.

Last week was kind of OK, in the end. I borrowed a gardening tool from Dad's shed at

Oak Hill – he didn't know but I'm sure he wouldn't have minded – and used it to tidy up the bench in my clearing. Dad said that as long as I didn't leave the grounds then he didn't really mind where I went – although then he spent half an hour giving me a long lecture on how I should be polite and helpful and friendly to anyone I met. He still hasn't noticed that I'm not talking when we're there. I worked really hard with the tool – it was like a massive pair of scissors – and now the bench is weed-free. It's the perfect place to sit and sketch and the hours passed really quickly every day.

I'm still dreading going back today, though. I've been begging Dad every morning to let me take Picasso with me, but he says there is a total no-animals rule at Oak Hill and there's no way he can come with us. Dad said that he'd lose his job for sure if he brought a dog into the grounds. It's a shame because if I had him with me then I think this could end up being a good summer after all.

I'm feeling quiet in the car and not really in the mood for conversation. Not that Dad would pick up on that in a million years. He thinks everything is fine between us. And that is just not true. I might have found a cool place to hang out at Oak Hill but that doesn't mean I've forgiven him for stealing my summer, any more than I've forgiven Mum for stealing my happiness.

As we get out of the car Dad is wittering on about a fence that needs repairing at the far end of the garden and I suddenly can't stand it any more. I feel like I'm just pretending to have a life this summer when really, it's impossible to be living when all your choices have been taken away from you. I follow Dad silently round the side of the house and watch as he gets his tools and tells me that he'll be on the north side of the garden if I need him.

Then I sink down on to the floor of the shed next to his bag and wonder if anyone else my age could possibly be feeling as desperate as I'm feeling right now. I can sense the holidays trickling through my fingers and there's not one single thing I can do to stop them. I'm going to go back to school in September and Lauren and Nat will have a whole summer of shared experiences and I'll have nothing to say.

I flop my head on to my knees and groan. The opportunities for rebellion are highly limited in this place. I suppose I could steal a wheelchair and take it for a spin? Or trample all over the flower beds? Not exactly dramatic. Nobody's going to be impressed with that when we go back to school.

I look around the shed, trying to find inspiration. I suppose it's a coincidence that inspiration finds ME by waving at me from Dad's workbag. I know, I know – I should have learnt my lesson the last time I stole from him but this is a bit different. Because he's not exactly in a position to get mad at me for this, unless he wants to be the world's biggest hypocrite.

When Mum was still part of our family, she made Dad promise that he would never smoke another cigarette as long as he lived. And he promised. He crossed his heart and hoped to die – which is what Mum said would happen if he didn't pack in the ciggies. But sticking out of the side pocket of his bag is an opened packet of Benson & Hedges – so he lied. And that means that he can't really have a go at me, not when he's my main role model these days. And anyway, I'll only take two so he'll never even notice they've gone.

I reach across and pull the packet out of the bag. Opening it up I see that it's three-quarters full. Perfect. Quickly I pull out two cigarettes and ram them into my pocket. Then I get up and walk to the door, running back at the last minute to take his lighter.

The sun is hotting up when I step out of the shed. Everyone's saying that this is the best summer on record since blah blah blah. I don't listen when they start talking about that – it just makes me crazy when I think about how I could be spending endless days at the park or the outside pool with Lauren and Nat. I'm in the mood for sketching and as I walk towards my hidden clearing I see another path that looks kind of interesting. I'm not in a rush so I walk down it to where it ends next to a water fountain. The fountain looks really old and is covered in green, yucky slime but I can still see how weird and amazing it is. Throwing my bag down on to a bench, I take out my sketchpad and start outlining the three stone tiers that are stacked like a wedding cake.

I've just got to the bottom level and am struggling to draw the strange goblin-like creatures that are holding up the base, when I hear voices. Looking around I see Beatrice, one of the care workers, pushing a wheelchair down the path. There's no time to make my escape because Beatrice has seen me and is making a beeline straight towards me, a big smile on her face. There's something about Beatrice that makes me think it would be a bad idea to annoy her. I've known her since I was little and she's always really nice but I get the feeling that she doesn't stand for any messing about.

'Here you are, lovely!' she beams. 'We've all been wondering where you've been disappearing to every day!'

I squeeze my lips together, desperately keeping the words inside so that I don't tell her about my secret hideaway. Beatrice doesn't notice, though – she's one of those people who will fill any silence with every thought that pops into her head.

'What a beautiful day,' she says, parking the wheelchair up next to my bench. 'Such a shame to waste it indoors! That's why I've brought Martha down here.' She sits next to me and claps her hands in joy. 'Look, Martha! Erin's drawn a picture. Oh – isn't that fantastic! How lovely!'

The strain of not running away is starting to get too much but before I can break Dad's rule and be completely unfriendly, a shrill beeping sound fills the air. Beatrice grabs her phone out of her pocket and looks at it, leaping off the bench as she reads the screen.

'Oh, goodness,' she mutters, turning to look first at Martha and then at me. 'Erin – can you do me a big favour, please?'

I don't have time to answer her before she rushes on.

'I'm needed back at the house. Will you stay here with Martha, just until I get back?' Beatrice turns away and starts back along the path.

'I'll be back as soon as I can. Thanks for helping out, Erin.' And then she is gone, leaving the stillness to flood back into the space left behind her.

I sit in stunned silence for a moment, feeling like a whirlwind has just passed through the garden. Then I turn and look at the inhabitant of the wheelchair for the first time. Martha. That's what Beatrice said she was called. She is sitting upright, facing straight ahead, with her legs tucked up tightly in a blanket and a silk scarf round her neck, despite it being scorching hot out here. I stare at her for a minute but she just keeps on looking at the fountain and I get the distinct impression that she doesn't want to be sitting next to me as much as I don't want to be sitting next to her.

Sighing, I turn back to my sketch but the enjoyment has gone since Beatrice said it was 'lovely'. I want to leave but Martha is so quiet and so old and Beatrice asked me to help her out by staying. And then I start to feel angry again, because I'm totally not responsible for some random old person who I don't even know and isn't even in my family. And I'm so angry that I want her to know that she means nothing to me – that even though she's an adult she's too old to be like a proper adult and she can't stop me from doing anything I want.

So I reach into my pocket and take out a cigarette and the lighter and I put the cigarette in my mouth and light it up, just like I've seen kids do in the park. And I take a deep breath and wait to see what all the fuss is about. I wait to see what it feels like to tell the world that I am in charge and that nobody can make me behave. And then I start coughing so hard that I think my stomach might actually come up through my mouth and tears are streaming down my face and I wonder if I might actually cough myself to death, here by this beautiful, freaky water fountain and this silent old woman.

It seems to take forever for me to stop choking and when I do I throw the cigarette on the floor and stamp on it with my trainer. Then I look across at Martha and wait for her to tell me that I'm too young to smoke and that she's going to tell my dad. But she doesn't say a word. Instead, she turns her head very slowly and looking me right in the eye, brings her left hand up to her face and mimes smoking.

I'm not sure what she means so I just stare back at her. She frowns at me and repeats the gesture, this time pointing at me and then back at herself, making it clear what she's asking.

'You want a cigarette?' I ask her and she nods, her head bobbing up and down. 'Sure,' I say, and reaching into my pocket I pull out the second stolen cigarette and hand it to her.

Martha takes the cigarette with a shaking hand and slowly, painstakingly, moves it up to her mouth. It dangles there between her lips and I am still for a moment, fascinated by the sight of her ruby-red lipstick. She has surprisingly nice lips for such an old person. Then she turns to me again and glares and I realize my mistake.

'Oh, sorry – you need a light.' She nods, her head barely moving and I pick up the lighter from the bench and gesture towards her. This just earns me another scowl, though, and I look at her in confusion – why is she such a grumpy old cow? I'm actually trying to be nice.

Martha's shoulders seem to slump forward and she slouches in her chair for a moment. Then she sits upright again and jerks her head in my direction, her chin pointing towards the lighter and I understand what she wants.

'OK, OK,' I mutter, flicking the lighter so that a small flame is flickering in the sunlight. 'Jeez – you must be used to being waited on around here.' I scoot across the bench. Martha leans towards me and I light her cigarette, watching as she inhales deeply and then breathes out, closing her eyes and relaxing back in her chair.

We sit like that for a while, and the silence is quite nice. After a bit, just when I'm wondering whether to continue with my sketch, there's the sound of footsteps coming down the pathway from the house. Martha and I must hear it at the same time because she spins her head in my direction, her eyes filled with something – I'm not sure if it's panic or amusement. I really, really don't want her to get caught smoking. There's bound to be questions about where she got the cigarette and I don't need the hassle. Her left hand is moving slowly towards her mouth but there's no time – she's too slow, so quick as a flash I reach across and yank the cigarette out from between her lips, grinding it into the gravel with my heel just as Beatrice appears in front of us.

'Have you two been having a lovely time?' she asks, her voice breaking our peaceful silence. I snort slightly – I only met Martha fifteen minutes ago but even I know that 'lovely times' are not really her thing. 'Thank you so much for helping out, Erin. I can see it's going to be handy, having you around this summer!'

I scowl at my feet. No way am I going to put myself in this situation again. What am I, a glorified old-person-sitter?

'Anyway, we don't want you getting too hot, do we, dear?' she says, moving behind Martha's wheelchair and taking hold of the handles. 'Time to say goodbye to Erin!'

She takes a step forward and then stops abruptly, staring down at the ground and then looking at me with eyes that have suddenly changed from jolly to distrustful.

'And *what* is this?' she demands, putting her nose in the air and sniffing like a dog. I look down and see the two cigarette butts, lying next to each other in front of us. 'Martha! We have had this conversation before. This is unacceptable behaviour. You have to start helping yourself – and this is NOT the way to do it!'

I glance across at Martha. She is sitting in her wheelchair and looking at me with an expression that I am finding hard to work out. Beatrice is ranting on behind her about how she's going to have to talk to the manager and how disappointed she is – she sounds like Dad when he's caught me doing something wrong. And then I see that Martha is smiling at me. It's not like a regular smile – her mouth isn't in the right shape at all, but if I look right into her eyes I could swear that they're laughing.

'I wouldn't be at all surprised if you're banned from time alone in the garden,' Beatrice is saying. 'You have to earn your trust, Martha – we told you that last time we had a *situation*.'

She says the word *situation* like it is something unpleasant, and I suddenly feel cross.

I've spoken before I've even thought it through properly.

'It's not like she's too young to smoke, though, is it? Can't she make her own choices?'

Beatrice looks at me in surprise and I shut up, instantly regretting my outburst.

'I guess I don't need to ask who provided Martha with the cigarettes.' Her eyes are piercing and I look down at the floor.

'Please don't tell my dad. He'll go mental if he finds out. It won't happen again, I promise.'

I look up to see Beatrice looking between Martha and me. She appears to be thinking. Martha just looks amused – silly old woman has no idea what's at stake here. I'm holding my breath – if Beatrice doesn't believe me then I'm in serious trouble. There's no way Dad will let me spend time alone after this. He might even send me off to Spain with Mum and her substitute family.

Then Beatrice looks down at the top of Martha's head, and she looks at me again and she shakes her head.

'Do I have your word that there will be no more smoking?' she asks. I nod furiously. 'That goes for BOTH of you,' she says, giving the wheelchair a little wiggle. Martha's eyes are dancing now and she looks like she might burst if she doesn't laugh soon.

Beatrice starts to push the wheelchair down the path.

'Martha will be out here again tomorrow afternoon if the weather stays fine,' she tells me. 'Just in case you're around.'

I watch as they retreat down the path, Beatrice's voice floating back to me as she tells Martha all about the bingo that's being organized for after supper. I have a little smile at the thought of Martha sitting in that living room, surrounded by people having fun. I'm getting the impression that Martha doesn't do what you expect old people to do. Beatrice is out of her mind if she thinks I'm hanging around anywhere near that crazy pensioner again. Martha's trouble and I definitely do not need anyone else ambushing my stupid summer.

TO THE UNKNOWN VOICE *

'I won't do it!' The words fly out of my mouth before Dad has even finished speaking. 'You can't be serious?'

'Calm down, Erin,' he says, stretching his legs out in front of him on the grass and reaching for another sandwich. 'You're completely overreacting. You never know, it might be fun!'

I stare at him in disbelief. Fun? Nothing about any of this could possibly be counted as 'fun'. I thought my summer couldn't get any worse but boy, was I wrong. Now, the thought of sitting on

* *To the Unknown Voice* (1916) by Wassily Kandinsky. Every time I look at this picture I see something different. I think you could use this watercolour and ink painting to tell a hundred stories, but never really know whose voice you can hear.

my own in my secret hideaway all day sounds blissful. Being lonely wasn't so bad.

'She's a snotty, up-herself, troublesome old lady,' I tell him. Dad raises an eyebrow and looks like he's trying not to smile, which just makes me madder. 'She didn't say one word to me yesterday. Why on earth would you think she'd want to spend time with me?'

'It was Beatrice's idea,' says Dad. 'She told me that the two of you got on splendidly yesterday and that it'd be really helpful if you could spend some time every day with Martha. And as I know how keen you are to show me that you're all mature and sensible now, I agreed that it was a good plan.'

Ah, now it all makes sense. We're being punished, Martha and me. Dad obviously doesn't know about the cigarettes and Beatrice is going to use this information to blackmail me into doing what she wants. My punishment is to help look after Martha, and Martha's punishment is to put up with me. Fantastic. What a great summer holiday this is turning out to be.

Dad throws me an apple and stands up. 'You're meeting her by the water fountain at two o'clock. Don't be late.' He starts to stride off across the garden, stopping by the hedge and turning back towards me. 'And keep an open mind, Erin.' Then he's gone and I am left scowling into thin air.

As I sit by the water fountain just before two o'clock, I think about Martha. She's not like any old person I've ever met before. She wasn't chatty and happy and interested in me like Granny Edna was. I'm not sure I've ever met such a grumpy pensioner before.

'Hello!' Beatrice calls to me as she pushes Martha through the sunshine and towards the bench where I am sitting. 'Good – you're here nice and early! Did your father explain the situation to you?'

I'm too scared of Beatrice's temper to ignore her so I nod. She parks Martha next to me and stands in front of the wheelchair, her hands on her hips and her face looking stern.

'Do not go leading this young lady astray – do you hear me?'

Martha looks at her blankly and Beatrice laughs – a loud, raucous laugh that makes me want to join in, despite my determination to be mad at her. 'Oh, you! Don't go giving me that dippy old lady routine. I'll be back in half an hour.

Behave.' She winks at me and saunters off down the path, whistling.

I look over at Martha. She's wearing her scarf again and a really daft floppy hat – it doesn't suit the moody scowl on her face one little bit and as I watch, she slowly reaches up her left arm and knocks the hat on to the floor.

'Shall I get that?' I say, bending down towards the ground. There is silence and when I look up, I see Martha glaring at me crossly. 'OK – I'll just leave it where it is, then,' I tell her, straightening up and leaning back on the bench. I don't blame her – it really is a stupid-looking hat.

We sit quietly for a while and then I see Martha shuffling around in her chair. I watch her lazily out of the corner of my eye, and see her reach under the blanket that tucks her legs in. It takes her ages because the blanket is wrapped round her really tightly, and she's only using her left hand. She must be left-handed like me. Eventually, she pulls back the blanket and takes out a notebook and pen. Then she stares off into the distance, completely in a world of her own. It's like she doesn't even know I'm here.

I ignore her right back and wonder if it's possible to die of boredom. Are we just supposed to sit here in silence for thirty minutes? It's certainly an effective punishment.

I sigh and start thinking about what Lauren and Nat will be doing right now. I saw on Facebook that they've been hanging out in the shopping centre and last week they swear that they went to the cinema with some boys from Year 11. I bet that isn't even true. I really hope it isn't, anyway.

A movement from Martha distracts me and I turn to look at her. She is trying to open the notebook, but her movements are really awkward and as I watch, she knocks it with her arm and it falls, landing on the ground next to the stupid hat.

I leap off the bench and crouch down, picking up the notebook and reaching for the pen that has rolled under her wheelchair.

'Here you go,' I say and pass them both back to her. She reaches out slowly and takes them from me but she still doesn't say a word. I wonder if she's a nun and has taken a vow of silence. Or maybe she just doesn't like me.

'O-K,' I say slowly. 'Just trying to help.'

I turn up the volume on my iPod and try to zone out but even though she isn't actually saying or doing anything, Martha is kind of hard to ignore. I close my eyes and start humming along to the song in an attempt to distract myself.

As the song finishes and the next one begins I get a prickling sensation down my spine. An unmistakable feeling that I am being watched. I open one eye and look across at Martha. She isn't gazing at the water fountain any more – instead, she's looking at me. She nods her head in that bossy way that means she wants me to do something and I turn off my iPod and sit up straighter. For an old woman she is totally rude – would it kill her to speak to me now and again? I have to admit, I'm curious, though. She's full of surprises.

This is certainly true right now. As I watch, Martha starts miming smoking a cigarette and glaring at me.

'Yeah, about that,' I tell her, feeling my face going red. 'I'm sorry if I got you into trouble yesterday.'

Martha scowls at me.

'You can't blame me entirely. It's not like I forced you to smoke it,' I say, feeling fed up. I'm just the child here – she's supposed to be the grown-up.

I'm about to turn my iPod back on when Martha holds something up. It's her notepad and she's written a word on the page. Her handwriting is horrible. There's no way she'd get away with writing like that in school nowadays. I wonder for a second about why she hasn't just spoken to me but then I read the word and get completely distracted.

Fag

Martha's eyebrows are raised expectantly and I understand now what she's been going on about. I snigger but the sound that comes out is all nervous and high-pitched.

'I haven't got any,' I say, wondering if she's going to start ranting and raving. Martha doesn't strike me as the sort of person to handle disappointment very well. She surprises me, though, and instead just does a sort of shrug and puts the notepad back down.

And we're back to sitting in silence again.

I've decided to utilize my time and get some of my art project done so I've looked through a couple of books and found the painting that I want to write about today. It's quite peaceful out here in the sunshine. I pick up my art book and start writing down my thoughts about a painting called *To the Unknown Voice*, but after a while I wonder if Martha might be getting bored. I think I'd better make some sort of effort in case she complains to Beatrice.

'So,' I say, 'how come you're at Oak Hill, then?'

Martha doesn't answer me, but her mouth turns down and I get the feeling that she isn't delighted to be here.

'Are you ever going to speak to me?' I ask her. 'This would all be a lot easier if you'd actually do some of the talking.' Martha scowls and looks away from me. I guess she doesn't like being told what to do, either.

'Is anyone coming to visit you today?' I'm determined to get her talking to me. I couldn't actually care less about what she's got to say but I don't like the fact that she's not saying anything. It's freaky – like she's playing a game and I don't know the rules. She shakes her head but at least she's actually looking at me now.

'What about tomorrow, then? Are your family coming then?' This is really hard work.

Martha shakes her head again. I'm starting to think that I'm asking the wrong questions here – that something isn't quite right.

'Martha – can you actually talk?' I ask, my voice a bit quieter than it was before. There's a long pause while Martha looks at me and I start to regret my question. Perhaps I've been rude. It's really none of my business, after all.

Just as I'm about to look away, Martha seems to make a decision about something. She looks up for a moment and when she looks back at me she shakes her head. Just once.

Then she bends over her notepad. She scrawls something on the page and then holds it up for me to see.

No FAMILY

That can't be right. Everybody has some kind of family. Even if they're really rubbish and run off and abandon you and don't care less about your happiness and what you really want. I slide along the bench so that I'm sitting closer to Martha.

'You mean you haven't got anyone?' I ask her.

She shakes her head.

'Did you never get married?'

Martha looks down at her hands for a minute and I follow her gaze. There, on the third finger of her left hand, all wrinkled and old, is a wedding ring.

'You were married!' I say, feeling pleased. I knew that it couldn't be true. Everybody has to have somebody.

Martha writes a note.

Tommy

I'm starting to enjoy this. It's a bit like a treasure hunt with the clues written down. I need more details, though, and I've got to work out the best questions to ask, seeing as Martha's voice doesn't seem to work properly.

'Where's Tommy now?'

Martha looks away and I feel the mood change. I've made a mistake asking that question.

'OK,' I rush, thinking fast. 'When did you meet him?'

Martha turns and points at me.

'When you were about my age? Wow – that must be years ago. So, you met Tommy when you were around twelve and later on you married him. Right?' Martha does her weird smiling face again. 'You must have really liked him then. I don't know any boys that I'd be prepared to marry!'

She scrawls two words on the notepad and I crane across her to read them.

No good

'Who was no good? Tommy?' I ask. She nods and sits up straight in her wheelchair. Then she writes again on her notepad. It takes her longer this time – she's really slow.

Let's go for a drive

What is she on about now? How are we supposed to go for a drive?

'I don't know what you mean,' I tell her slowly, feeling an uncomfortable feeling creeping over me. Martha does her weird grin again and mimes driving a car. Oh no. I don't think so.

'Er, Martha? You do know I'm not even thirteen yet, don't you?' I ask her. 'I can't actually drive a car.'

Martha points at herself and I try not to let the laugh that bubbles up out of me escape but I just can't help it.

'You? You want me to help you go for a drive? Are you actually serious?'

Martha scrunches up her nose and wiggles her head from side to side as if she is mocking me. It's the sort of face that Lauren makes when Nat says something ridiculous, and seeing Martha do it makes me feel properly annoyed.

'Fine!' I tell her. 'We'll just roll on over to the car park and pick a car we fancy the look of, shall we?' I can hear my voice sounding really sarcastic and rude and I'm slightly shocked at how I'm talking to this woman that I barely even know. There's just something about her that makes me feel – I don't know – maybe a bit nervous but adventurous and brave at the same time. I know I wouldn't have got away with talking to Granny Edna like this, that's for sure – Mum would have had a fit.

Martha writes a note.

DAD'S VAN

I lean back on the bench and look at her. I cannot believe that she has just said that. An octogenarian is encouraging me to joyride. My summer just got even more random.

'You are out of your mind,' I tell her and then I watch as Martha's shoulders start shaking, her dimpled cheeks start wobbling and her eyes shine over with unshed tears. She is laughing. And her laughter may be silent but it is powerful. Any other time I'd be joining in, but not today. Not now. Today I am suddenly furious with the ancient, withered old woman in front of me. What business does she have suggesting things like that to me?

'Oh, grow up. You're old enough to know better.' She's making me feel stupid, like I'm the responsible one and she's the little kid and I don't like it.

I've said the right thing to get her attention. She's not laughing any more and as I watch, she pulls herself up so that she seems to tower over me, even though she's still sitting in the wheelchair.

She fixes me with her suddenly steely eyes, making me feel like I'm pinned down to the bench. Then she writes again and thrusts the notepad towards me.

GROW OLD - YES. GROW UP - NEVER

I can see the disgust on her face. I look away and think about this. What on earth is she on about – never growing up? She's about as old as it's possible to get so she *must* be grown up.

She's definitely grown old, though, that's for sure. I glance back at her, sitting in her wheelchair, and see her hands are all twisted. She reminds me of an old oak tree, all ancient and gnarled. I peer at her closely, this time trying to *really* look at her. But even if I focus really hard and squint my eyes a bit, I can't see someone like me. It's just too difficult – what with all the wrinkles and baggy skin. Maybe her eyes look like they could belong to a naughty, adventurous teenager but the rest of her is one hundred per cent old lady. It's weird, actually – like her eyes aren't connected to the rest of her body. A bit like an invasion of the bodysnatchers.

It makes me wonder if the real, young, fun Martha is hiding inside the old worn-out body sitting next to me. A Martha who thinks that stealing my dad's van is a good idea. A Martha who wants to get out of here. But this is such a weird thought that I shake my head and look back at the water fountain. Martha is just an old woman. Unable to cook her own meals or dress herself properly or even talk like a normal person. An old woman sitting here waiting for her time to come to an end.

Martha doesn't want to talk now and I'm glad.

When Beatrice returns, Martha is dozing in her wheelchair.

'Everything all right?' whispers Beatrice to me.

'I think so,' I whisper back, because honestly – how would I even know if Martha wasn't all right? It's not like I'm a doctor or a care person or something. I wonder for a moment if I should tell Beatrice about Martha's desire to joyride but decide there's no point. It was probably just a weird old-person joke, anyway, and I don't want to get her into trouble, even if she is a pain.

'Thank you for spending time with Martha,' says Beatrice. 'It's lovely to see her out here with someone. She's usually on her own and I worry about her being lonely.'

'No problem,' I mutter but meanly I'm thinking that it's not like I had an actual choice. I guess I hardly have to do anything. Just sit in silence with someone who can't even talk to me but has no problem with asking me to break the law. All in a day's work.

'And it sorts two problems at once, which is good,' continues Beatrice. 'There was I, wondering what to do about Martha, and there was your dad, wondering what to do about you. It's all worked out perfectly!'

Beatrice is still talking but I'm suddenly so cross that I can hardly bring myself to reply to her. Martha stirs and wakes and I can feel her eyes on me. When I glance in her direction it feels like she's asking me a question. For a second, I can tell that she knows something is wrong – but I turn my head away. She wouldn't get it. She wouldn't understand that right now, I feel as if not one single person in the entire world cares about how I spend my summer. God – Martha probably thinks she's doing me a *favour* by hanging out with me. This isn't right. I need to take control of this situation.

I don't look at Martha once when Beatrice starts arranging for us to meet up again tomorrow. I'm not sure why I don't tell her the truth – which is that I totally can't stand old people. That ridiculous suggestion about taking my dad's van for a drive – it's just wrong. It's MY generation who should be talking about that sort of thing – not hers. Martha is antique. That's not what old people *do*. And all that rubbish about growing up but not growing old. She's grown old so she must have grown up. News flash – that's what happens. You don't get to choose. I can't tell Beatrice that I don't want to be with *anybody*, especially not silent Martha, because she'd ask why and I don't have an answer that's good enough for her. I don't think she'd want to hear that I feel betrayed. That I don't need any help finding my own friends and even if I actually *am* a bit lonely then I'd rather have nobody than someone who smells like death.

I wonder if one day I'll be trapped, like Martha is, inside wrinkly skin and a dilapidated shell. And I think that this summer is bad enough without people coming up with new and imaginative ways to make me miserable.

MARTHA

The girl, Erin, asked me about Tommy. I'd been trying to ignore her in the hope that she would go away and leave me in peace, but she was quite insistent for a young thing. It was my own fault really, for writing her the note. I just thought that she might possibly have some more cigarettes and contraband like that is very hard to come by in this prison that masquerades as a care home. I'd have happily ignored her all day but then she asked about family. She asked about Tommy. She wanted to know when I met him. It has been years since I thought about that day but now, sitting here with nothing else to entertain me, it's all coming back.

The rain is pouring down outside and the clouds make the night so dark. It was very different that particular day. Then the sun shone and there wasn't a cloud in the sky. That was why it seemed like such a good idea when Tommy invited me to go to the woods with him.

Oh, it wasn't the first time that I met him. We'd been at school together ever since we were little ones. But it was only that summer that I'd started to see him differently. It was only that summer that I really noticed him. I was thirteen years old so it must have been the summer of 1942.

My younger sister, Mim, was the biggest cause of trouble in my life at that time. She didn't make the trouble (I did that all by myself) but she always seemed to be around somewhere, waiting for me to do something wrong. If only she hadn't felt the need to follow me home from school that day then everything would have been fine. It would have been more than fine, in fact. It would have been perfect.

It was my own fault. I should have thought to check. I allowed myself to get carried away in the excitement and when Tommy asked me to cycle down to the woods with him I could think of nothing but he and I, together and alone.

He'd been asking me all week. I said no for the first four days but by that day I was getting worried that he'd give up on me and ask Margaret instead. I knew that she would say yes in a flash. She was a bit brazen like that. So I agreed to go and we were getting along really well until my horrid, frightful sister decided to follow us. She waited until we had got off our bicycles and were just inside the wood. Tommy was pointing out a bird sitting high up in the tree above us and then his arm was round my shoulder and I was fairly certain that my first kiss was about to happen. I was just thinking how glad I was that I would always be able to remember this moment – Tommy and the sunlight trickling through the branches, making the whole world look enchanted and magical.

Everything was completely right and I was just wondering whether it was time to close my eyes and lean in for his kiss when there was a horrendous, screeching sound. Tommy and I sprang apart and when we looked round, there was Mim, halfway across the field and standing up on the pedals of her bicycle so that she could see more clearly.

I knew I could never catch her but I had to try. I left Tommy standing on his own in the wood. It wasn't the only time that I would do that to him and the second time it happened, the memory of this day made it all the harder.

It was too late, though. By the time I raced into the backyard, Mother was standing in the doorway, wiping her floury hands on her apron, looking furious. Mim was loitering behind her with a rotten kind of smirk on her face.

Mother wouldn't listen when I told her that nothing had happened. She said that nice girls like me did not go within spitting distance of the woods with the likes of Tommy McGregor. She said that he was 'No Good', and that I was a terrible role model for Mim. I was banned from going anywhere except home and school for the next two weeks and told that it was about time I started to grow up.

I didn't really care about that and I didn't pay much attention to what she said to me, either. I didn't care about getting older and I thought that growing up sounded like a very dull sort of thing to be bothered with.

Oh, I'm not daft. I've got eyes. When I look in the mirror I can see the old lady I've become. Age cannot be halted and only a fool would try to stop time from doing its duty. After all, there are *some* perks.

Growing up, however, is a different matter altogether. Nobody ever tells you that this is purely optional. How you behave is completely at your own discretion and I, for one, intend to do as I please. My advanced years do provide me with certain benefits, you see. Nobody suspects the elderly of being capable of anything other than knitting bootees for babies and sucking on toffees. I have found a certain freedom in this.

But oh, my poor, No-Good Tommy. If only that picture of him, standing in the dappled sunlight under the trees that day was the last memory I had of him. If this were so then I think I would be a happy woman. The girl asked me where he is now. I wish I had the answer to that question, although I suspect I shall discover it before too long.

I would like to see her again, despite her incessant need to talk. Her questions have reminded me of things that I thought were buried long ago. I think she might be fun. She might help to liven things up a bit.

GRANNIES*

The last two days have been totally boring. I don't know how Dad doesn't go mad, hanging around the garden all day. Plants are seriously dull.

I've done my penance and met up with Martha at the agreed time each day. I've barely spoken to Dad about her, except after that first afternoon when he asked me if we'd had a nice chat. I

* *Grannies* (2006) by Banksy. We did a whole topic last year in school about whether graffiti could ever be classed as art. This was one of my favourite pictures. The two grannies are working so hard at their knitting and it's only when you see the words that they are knitting into their jumpers that you start to think. The granny writing 'thug for life' looks like my Granny Edna. It's kind of hard to imagine an old person being a thug but that's what this picture makes you do. I suppose it isn't just young people that can behave badly.

laughed quite a lot at that until he got cross with me.

We've sat in complete silence on both days – I listen to my iPod and do my sketching and don't bother talking to her. She's probably glad that she can just be moody and miserable without any interruptions because it's not like she's tried to get my attention or anything. On the positive side, I've done some great sketches. On the negative side, my voice is going to forget how to work if I don't find someone to talk to soon.

I've thought a few times about Martha and Tommy. She met him when she was my age and then ended up marrying him. It's made me think about the boys I know. I reckon I must be the least popular girl in Year 8. Nobody has shown the slightest interest in even wanting to go out with me, so based on that evidence there's a strong possibility that I may never actually get married. Not that anyone at school knows that I've never had a boyfriend. Not even Lauren and Nat. Everyone has gone a bit mental with the whole boy-girl thing. Four different boys asked Lauren out just on one day (and she said yes to each of them). It can be kind of hard to concentrate in lessons with the amount of asking out that's always going on. I get jabbed in the back with a ruler at least three times in every maths lesson and every time I turn round there'll be a note being thrust in my face. Always with someone else's name on the front.

When it all first started I used to joke that it was all good work experience for if I want to get a job delivering the mail when I grow up. Which I absolutely do not. But after a while I started to feel left out, which I guess was natural when the entire year group was in a whirlwind dating frenzy and I was left standing in the middle like an abandoned bit of tumbleweed. Even Shelley, who has got really bad spots (not to be mean or anything but it's true), got asked out at the end-of-term disco.

That pushed me over the edge. I was completely fed up with being the only person in the whole of Year 8 without a boyfriend. And that was when Barney entered my life. He was in Year 10 and went to school in a different town. Barney was completely head over heels in love with me, right from the beginning.

I enjoyed showing Lauren and Nat the bead bracelet that he bought me to celebrate our two-week anniversary. He was such a softie and totally romantic. I told my friends to keep it a secret, that I didn't want anyone to find out I was dating an older boy. That ensured that everyone in my French class knew about it before lunchtime and by the end of the day I was the talk of Year 8.

It was fantastic! Barney was generous and funny and obviously, drop-dead gorgeous. He had black, curly hair and sparkling blue eyes and his favourite thing of all was to write love songs about me that he would play on his guitar. Best of all, he thought that I was the most amazing girlfriend that a boy could possibly have.

'He sounds too good to be true,' said Nat dreamily, every time I mentioned him. She had no idea how right she was.

Yes – Barney was perfect in every way. The problems only began when Lauren and Nat started demanding to meet him. Then, his lack of existence became a bit of an issue and I had to think quickly.

So one rainy Monday morning I went to school looking sad. It was over, I told my friends. Barney was just getting too needy. He wanted more from me than I was prepared to give and the final crunch had come over the weekend when he said that I was spending too much time with Lauren and Nat.

They were utterly horrified. They dried my tears and held my hand and together we made a pact.

'Mates before dates,' we said. No way would we ever let a boy tear our friendship apart. Lauren and Nat even dumped their boyfriends in a show of solidarity and we spent all our spare time together for the next week, listening to music and reading magazines and slagging off all the boys we knew. Then life got back to normal – they got asked out and I was left passing messages of undying love (at least until morning break) from one end of the classroom to the other.

If Mum was more interested, then I suppose that I could ask her why no boys seem to like me. I could ask her what other people see when they look at me. When I look in the mirror I just see me. An ordinary person. I mean, my hair's a bit of a state – it's kind of a blackish mop stuck on top of my head, and my nose has got a bit of a bump in the middle and I'm quite short for my age but I'm not hideous or anything. Maybe it's my personality that's the problem. Perhaps I'm just the sort of person that other people don't want to be around? Mum could probably answer that one really easily but I'm definitely not going to ask her. I'm scared of what she might say.

Then again, Mum wouldn't understand even if I did ask her opinion. She's got two men that want to be with her. What would she know about feeling lonely and unattractive and unwanted? And there's no way I can ask Dad – he'd have an actual heart attack if I started talking about emotions and feelings and stuff and I'd die of complete humiliation.

I've been in the hideaway all morning, eaten a silent lunch with Dad and am now dragging my sorry self towards the water fountain, ready for yet another thrilling afternoon of boredom. As I walk down the pathway from Dad's shed I suddenly see Martha and Beatrice rounding the hedge ahead of me, on the path that leads to the fountain. I fling myself off the path and hide behind a bush, desperate not to be spotted. I realize that this is a bit ridiculous but my punishment time doesn't start until I reach the bench and I don't intend to prolong the agony by walking there with the pair of them, Beatrice all chatty and Martha all moody.

Suddenly I feel goose bumps on the back of my neck, as if somebody is watching me. I turn my head slowly and stifle a shriek as I see a pair of big eyes peering at me from behind a tree. Then I relax. It's just one of Dad's sculptures. I haven't seen this one before and it's actually really realistic, in a freaky way. He's used a knobbly bit of old tree trunk to create a weird, lizard-type creature that looks as if it's about to scuttle off into the undergrowth. Mum was right – Dad is pretty good at this stuff.

I turn back to my bush and peep through the leaves, breathing a sigh of relief as I watch Beatrice and Martha head away from me, the wheelchair crunching over the gravel towards the fountain.

Once they're out of sight I get up, brushing bits of twig and leaves off my legs and feeling a bit foolish. Then I follow them down the path, walking as slowly as I can, keen to prolong my freedom for a few more minutes.

Beatrice is quick to leave once I've reached the water fountain and I sink on to the bench without even glancing in Martha's direction. God, it's so utterly dull around here. There is exactly nothing to do and nobody worth talking to. I think about the rest of the summer holidays, stretching away into the distance with no end in sight and I start to feel desperate. I can't just sit on this bench for the next four weeks. I'll actually go stark staring crazy.

And then my phone beeps. Pulling it out of my pocket I see a text message from Nat.

OMG!!! U HAVE TO RING ME NOW!!! U WON'T
BELIEVE WHAT JUST HAPPENED!!!

The buzz of excitement in my stomach has less to do with the shouty capitals and more to do with the fact that something has happened. Something unexpected. Finally! I scroll to Nat's name in my contacts list and press dial. And my stupid, lame phone loses signal.

No – this is not fair. I've done everything everyone has asked of me. I've spent every weekday at Oak Hill and I'm generously giving my own free time to looking after a grouchy old woman. Surely I'm paying my dues?

I wave my phone in the air, but nothing happens. This is a critical situation – time critical. If I don't ring Nat now then she won't bother to text me next time and I won't have a clue about what's going on because she'll tell Lauren instead and I'll be even more on the outside than I already am. I have to make this call.

I leap on to the bench but it's no good. The water fountain is surrounded by trees and I think they might be blocking the signal or something. Holding my phone in front of me like a person searching for water with a divining rod, I step off the bench and walk slowly forward towards the other side of the fountain. Nothing.

There's a path that I haven't been down before on the other side and I head towards the end, passing between hedges and under trees. And then, finally, just as I'm starting to think that there is no hope, my phone beeps and I've got three bars of signal. Not great, but hopefully enough to make a call. I cross my fingers as the phone rings and when I hear Nat's voice on the other end I nearly shout with happiness.

'Nat! Tell me what's going on!' I screech.

'Is that you, Erin?' Nat's voice sounds a long way away.

'Yes! What's the big news?'

'You totally won't believe it!' she shrieks, and then my phone cuts out again.

'No!' I cry, waving it frantically in the air. Why is my life so rubbish? Is it really too much to ask that I have a bit of happiness every now and again?

I take a step forward, determined to find signal again if it kills me, but a noise from behind stops me in my tracks.

I turn, but the only things I can see are hedges. Perhaps I was mistaken? But then I hear it again – a faint cry in the distance. It's quiet and frail and unmistakably human. And it's coming from the direction of the water fountain.

Shoving my phone into my pocket I start to run, dodging small bushes and rounding hedges as fast as I can. As I burst out on to the gravel area round the fountain I see three things. The first is Martha's notepad, lying on the ground. The second is her wheelchair, tipped over on its side with one wheel still slowly turning and the third is Martha, sprawled next to it and making a sound unlike any I've ever heard before.

I freeze, my feet skidding and making the gravel spray up over my trainers. For a second I lock eyes with Martha, her cheek pressed against the ground. The look in her eyes makes me feel something new. Something unwelcome. I did this. I left her on her own when I was supposed to be looking out for her.

I blink and start to take a step forward but before I can move I'm shoved to one side as somebody blurs past me.

'Hey!' he shouts, sprinting over to her and kneeling down on the ground. 'Are you OK? What happened?'

My brain seems to have entered a planet all of its own because I am making no sense of the scene in front of me. It's him. The boy I met in town the day that I bought the iPad. I have no idea why he's here and I don't know what to do about Martha but my feet are doing the thinking for themselves and suddenly I'm standing over the pair of them.

The boy looks up at me. 'Go and get some help,' he tells me and while he's speaking quietly I can hear the fear in his voice. 'And be quick.'

I stand for another moment, looking at Martha lying on the ground. She doesn't seem so formidable now – just small and vulnerable. Guilt is churning around my stomach and I don't think I can leave her again – but then the boy glances back up at me.

'Go!' he orders and I go, running away from the fountain and down the path towards the house.

When I think about it later, I can see that logically, it only took a few minutes to track down Beatrice and tell her what had happened. It didn't feel like just a few minutes, though. It felt like hours. When I followed the care workers back to the fountain my heart felt as if it was going to bang right out of my chest. What if Martha died? That happened to old people, right? They couldn't cope with falling over – something to do with their bones being really weak or something. If Martha died it'd be all my fault because I left her alone.

But she wasn't dead. Beatrice and the other care workers got her upright and then slowly, carefully lifted her into the wheelchair. The boy had moved off to the other side of the bench and I was too ashamed to look at him – scared about what I'd see on his face. As the quiet, solemn procession headed down the path I shrank back under the trees. This wasn't the place for me, not now.

MARTHA

I tend to believe that old worn-out clichés are genuinely a complete load of bunkum and today has proved me right, yet again. *With experience comes wisdom.* I've never heard of anything so ridiculous in my life. I have lived for eighty-five years and had a great many experiences but I am no closer to being wise than I was as a girl of twelve.

Erin is self-centred, self-absorbed and only interested in her own needs. Normally I would applaud those characteristics but she has overstepped the mark today. She failed to keep her word and that is a trait I refuse to accept in even my closest friends. I suppose, here, I must acknowledge that I no longer have any close friends, but that's not the point. There are rules and while I, possibly more than the next person, believe that rules were made to be broken, there is no excuse for breaking a promise. She agreed to stay with me in the garden and she wandered off at the first opportunity. No backbone, that's her problem.

I must admit to feeling a little sad when she turned up at the water fountain and refused to speak to me. I had hoped that her chattering would provide me with some entertainment. Instead I've had to listen to Beatrice, who means well but is overworked and underpaid and gives out a perpetual aura of exhaustion. I have enough exhaustion in my life – what I crave, what I need, is youth and verve and enthusiasm. Zest for life and couldn't-care-less. The girl has all of that flowing out from her in waves. She has enough to share.

I've been thinking about my childhood since Erin asked me those questions the other day. It's funny, the things that you remember. Growing up in the war, you'd think it was all terror and misery, but we children just didn't see things like that. I remember being given our gas masks and Mim and I having to practise putting them on. They were hot and smelt of rubber, which I loathed. I couldn't see the point of carrying them around with me everywhere I went. I had no fear of death. Death wasn't something that happened to children, or so I thought in the early days.

I hated the gas mask – although I loved the small cardboard box that we were supposed to keep it in. It had a long strap that I wore over my shoulder and if I took the gas mask out and hid it under my bed, there was room in the box for my penknife and a pencil and an apple. I used to imagine it was my handbag.

Of course, Mim cottoned on to what I was up to and reported me to Father. He was furious and I had to present myself to him every evening at 6 p.m. for gas-mask checks.

Death wasn't something that was part of my life until the summer that I was fourteen years old. I was playing with my friends in the field behind our house when a German plane, obviously in trouble, swooped right low down by us, preparing to land. I could see the pilot's face through the cockpit window and my feet just wouldn't move. They were rooted to that field as if I was wearing a pair of concrete boots – there was no chance of getting out of his way. Everything happened very quickly. My friends were screaming and I saw him looking at us, and then he zoomed up again into the sky, only to crash into the next field where his plane burst into flames. I have often wondered if his mother knew of his bravery and the way he sacrificed himself to save his enemy's children.

It surprises me, when I've been remembering, to look in the mirror. In my memories I am a young (and rather beautiful) girl. The reality is shocking and it can take me a moment to work out who the wrinkled old woman is that appears to be standing by my shoulder. The problem is that everyone from the old days has gone – there is nobody left to see the Martha who was young, full of energy and love. Only I know that I'm still here inside.

LOOKING BACK TO A
BRIGHT FUTURE*

It's Saturday and we're back at Oak Hill. Dad had the chance of some overtime and when he asked if I minded I told him that it didn't really matter to me – being grounded in the house is just as bad as being grounded at Oak Hill. I think he looked a bit sad when I said that but I don't care – I hope he feels guilty for wrecking my summer.

Nobody has said a word to me about what happened the other day with Martha. I turned up

* *Looking Back to a Bright Future* (2003) by Julie Mehretu. This artist makes massive pictures on huge canvases using ink and acrylics. When I look at this painting it makes me feel that there might be good things ahead but that getting there could be difficult. It makes me wonder if it's really worth all the effort?

at the water fountain as usual the day after but she didn't appear. I expected to get hauled in front of Dad and given a hard time, but it's like nobody knows that I abandoned her. Almost as if she didn't tell anyone, which I find difficult to believe because I definitely get the impression that she can't stand me. She could have written it down in her notebook and shown Beatrice.

After saying goodbye to Dad at his shed I race through the gardens, heading straight for my secret hideaway. A whole day on my own will be good – I could do with some peace and quiet after all the excitement of this week.

I run round the corner and screech to a halt. There is somebody here. In MY hideaway. I haven't spotted a single person here all summer but now I can see somebody crouched down in the long grass by the stream. I stand still, unsure whether to turn and run before I'm spotted or march over there and tell them to get lost.

Before I can make up my mind, the figure stands up and looks straight at me.

'Hey!' he calls. 'Come and see this!'

He crouches back down in the grass and I walk forward slowly, staring at him in disbelief. *It's him again*. The gorgeous, scruffy-haired boy. The one that raced in to rescue Martha the other day. Why is he HERE, in my secret place? Maybe he's come to have a go at me about leaving Martha all alone. I make a pathetic attempt to smooth my hair down as I get closer to him and wish that I wasn't wearing my old jeans and a ratty T-shirt.

He looks up as I get close.

'Look! It's so cool!'

I look where he's pointing and my first instinct is to recoil in horror. It is not cool. It is disgusting. There, right next to gorgeous boy, is the ugliest, wartiest frog that I have ever seen. Not to mention the biggest.

'I haven't seen one this size before,' he says, sounding excited. I sigh, feeling disappointed. There's always something to spoil it. He might look stunning and seem kind of friendly – but he's obviously a total weirdo.

'Er – no,' I say. 'Me neither. But then again, I don't exactly go out of my way to look for frogs.'

'It's not a frog!' he says, laughing and standing up. 'It's a toad.'

'Oh – I'm so sorry. My bad. Frog – toad. Whatever.'

I'm aware that I'm not being very friendly but I'm seriously put out that someone else has intruded into my personal space – even if he is really good-looking. Plus I'm getting ready to defend myself if he starts blaming me for Martha's fall.

'I'm Lucas,' says Frog Boy. 'We go to the same school, don't we? You're about to start Year Nine, right?'

He holds out his hand and it takes me a moment to realize that he wants us to shake hands. I hesitate – if he's been touching that frog then I have no intention of getting slime on me and anyway, who shakes hands in this day and age?

'It's OK,' he tells me. 'I haven't got *toady* hands.' And then he grins at me and I find myself putting my hand in his – this strange, mind-reading, gorgeous Frog Boy.

'You must be Erin,' he says and I feel my insides lurch. Maybe he is actually psychic. I really hope he didn't read my mind when I was thinking mean thoughts about him.

'Yeah,' I say. I am not behaving like a particularly sophisticated young lady right now but thankfully, Frog Boy either hasn't noticed or doesn't care.

'My grandad told me about you,' he says and we start walking through the grass towards the bench that I spent hours clearing. 'I've been looking out for you for a while – I mean, Grandad's great and everything but when him and Mum start rambling on about the old times I do get a bit bored. I thought I'd tracked you down the other day but then we had to deal with Martha falling out of her chair. By the way, sorry if I sounded bossy – it's just that you looked so freaked-out and I knew we needed to get some help! And today I stumbled upon this place – I guess I've found your hidden lair!'

'I guess so,' I mutter weakly.

'You come here every day, right?' continues Frog Boy. I nod – he seems to have stolen my voice. 'Cool! Mum wants to visit Grandad loads over the next few weeks because she's taken some time off work. We can hang out.'

We've reached the seat and for the first time in the last few minutes, Frog Boy seems unsure of himself. 'I mean, only if you want to. I don't want to invade your space or anything.'

I look at him, my brain trying to think straight. I don't know why, but I just can't seem to say the right thing to this boy and, even with his weird frog fixation, I think that I might like him. But I'm messing it up and now he's smiling at me and nodding a bit and walking away, and in two seconds he's going to have gone round the corner and out of sight, and I'll have missed my chance.

'I'd like that!' I suddenly call. 'Hanging out, I mean. I'll be here on Monday afternoon.'

Frog Boy grins again and holds up a hand to wave goodbye. I wave weakly back in reply and it is only then, as I watch him disappear down the path, that I have two thoughts. One: that he doesn't seem to know that Martha's fall was my fault, and Two: that he held my hand all the way from the frog to the seat. And I didn't even notice.

FAIRY TALE *

I spend most of Sunday planning my outfit for Monday and my meeting with Frog Boy. (I know he told me his name but I totally can't remember it so I'm hoping it just kind of comes up in conversation.) It needs to be fabulous but completely casual – like I've chucked on some old clothes but still look amazing. In the end I settle for skinny jeans and my short-sleeved check shirt. Mum used to say that the purple and black in the shirt brought out the dark brown in my eyes. I don't know if that's true but it's always been my favourite top since she said that.

* *Fairy Tale* (1944) by Hans Hoffmann. I think that this looks like two arms, creating a messy, complicated, world. It's called *Fairy Tale* because it's full of fear and dark forces and winding pathways that never lead anywhere. It shows the uselessness of looking for a happy ending.

I think I must be quite distracted because Dad asks me if I'm OK at least three times. I tell him I'm fine but I don't think he believes me. I've shown Picasso my outfit and I think he approved. It was kind of hard to tell, though, because all he seems to want to do is sleep at the moment. He's getting seriously lazy.

I get to the secret hideaway before Frog Boy and wander down to the stream, lying on my stomach and dangling my fingers in the water, watching the sunlight reflect off the ripples and make funny patterns on the stones.

'Looking for your frog?' A voice yanks me out of my doze and I look up, squinting into the sun.

'Huh?' I say, carrying on the tradition of behaving like a complete idiot in front of this boy.

Frog Boy sinks down on to the grass beside me.

'Looking for your frog? You know, the one you have to kiss to turn him back into a prince so that you can live happily ever after!'

'Yeah, well,' I say, turning back to the stream, 'I'm kind of over *happily ever after*s. Turns out they don't even exist.'

'Yeah. *Happily ever after* should be sued by the Trade Descriptions Act,' agrees Frog Boy, picking a piece of grass and holding it between his thumbs. Then he cups his hands together and blows into them, making a high-pitched, whistling sound.

'Hey! How do you do that?' I ask, scrambling up on to my knees. We spend the next twenty minutes with him trying to teach me, but the only sound I can make is a farty, raspberry noise – nothing like the shrill squeal that he can do.

By the time I give up we're laughing and chatting as if we've known each other forever. I can't remember feeling like this around a boy before – like I can just be myself and not pretend to be someone I'm not.

In fact, I'm so chilled out that when I see the shadow being made by a tree across the stream, I don't think twice about pulling my sketchbook out of my rucksack. Normally I'd never let anyone see it, just in case they thought I was rubbish. I sit, cross-legged in the grass, and start drawing and even though I've only just met him, I'm pretty sure that Frog Boy won't mock me.

He doesn't say anything for a while, but after ten minutes or so he scoots closer to me and peers over my shoulder.

'That's really good,' he tells me, and I feel myself flush with pride. 'I like the way you've used the pencil lightly – almost like I have to imagine what might fill in the gaps.'

I look round at him. 'Do you like art too?' I ask. He laughs.

'Like it? Sure. Am I any good at it? No chance.' He lies back on the grass and looks up at the clouds, skittering across the sky as if they're in a hurry to get somewhere before dark.

'I bet you *are* good. You probably just don't know it,' I say. I want to make him feel good too, like he's made me feel.

'No. Seriously, I'm terrible at art. If I try to draw a cat everyone thinks it's a hamster. On steroids. I got an A for effort and an F for achievement on my last school report.'

I wince. That is pretty awful. Frog Boy sees my face and grins at me again.

'Don't worry about it. Art just isn't my thing. What I love more than anything is writing.'

I leap on this with enthusiasm. 'Ooh – what sort of thing do you write? I bet you're great.'

He sits up and looks at me carefully, his big blue eyes looking as if they're trying to decide something. 'Well . . .' he says slowly, 'I have got this one idea for a book that I think could be huge.'

'Go on!' I say, totally focused on every word. My mind is already racing ahead – he could write a book and I could do the illustrations. How cool would *that* be?

'OK, I'll tell you. But you have to swear you'll keep it a secret.'

'I swear,' I breathe. There's something about Frog Boy that makes me believe he could do anything he wanted.

He looks down at the grass and then peeks up at me through his eyelashes, making himself look even more adorable than usual. He has every single bit of my attention.

'It's about a boy,' he starts.

'Go on,' I say.

'It's about a boy who goes to boarding school.' He pauses. 'A magical boarding school for wizards.'

'Hang on –' I say, starting to feel suspicious.

'Let me finish!' interrupts Frog Boy. 'I haven't got to the best bit yet. Don't you WANT to hear my idea for a bestselling novel?'

I nod, deciding to give him the benefit of the doubt.

'As I was saying, it's about a boy who goes to a magical boarding school for wizards. His name (and this is the genius part), his name is – Gary Botter!'

Frog Boy erupts into laughter as he watches my face. I thump him on the arm.

'You are such an idiot,' I tell him, trying really hard not to snigger.

'Come on, though – I totally had you,' he says, lying back on the grass.

'Not even close,' I tell him, lying next to him on my stomach with my hands under my chin. 'You'll have to do a lot better than that to fool me.'

The sun is still hot and it's totally silent except for the sound of the breeze blowing through the leaves and the stream flowing over the stones. I'm not sure I've ever been anywhere this peaceful in my whole life and I think it'd be nice to stay here and not have to worry about other people and how they're feeling.

'So, what's the deal with Martha, then?' asks Frog Boy suddenly, ruining my chilled vibe.

'What d'you mean?' I think it's best if I play it cool until I've figured out what he knows.

'Well, my grandad told me that you were hanging out with her, but you haven't even been into the house to visit her since she fell. She's fine, by the way – just a few bumps and bruises.'

I redden and say nothing. It hadn't even dawned on me to visit her. I'd be the last person she'd want to see.

'Grandad thought it was a shame. He said you were good for her.'

I look at Frog Boy in disbelief. 'Good for her? She hates me. She probably never wants to see me ever again.'

Frog Boy looks at me with a weird expression on his face. 'Er, OK . . .' he says slowly, drawing out the syllables of each word. 'Not sure where you're getting your information but Grandad reckons she really likes you.'

I don't know what to think about this. It makes no sense. 'What do you mean?' I say. 'She's completely grumpy and miserable whenever I see her.'

Frog Boy laughs.

'Oh, she is,' he tells me. 'Super-grumpy. Grandad always says that if there were an award for grouchiest pensioner then Martha would win hands down. But he only says it to make her scowl. He likes her really. And he said that she definitely frowned less after she'd had a visit from you. That's why he thought you were good for her. Gave her something to think about.'

I don't know what to say to this. I think for a while but my thoughts are all jumbled up and I can't seem to work out what I should do next. I groan and roll on to my back, looking up at the clouds and wishing that, just for once, life could be simple.

'What's wrong?' asks Frog Boy. He has heard my groan and propped himself up on one arm, looking down at me.

'I wasn't actually that nice to Martha,' I tell him. 'I thought that she – well, anyway, it doesn't matter what I thought. I didn't really think about her at all, I guess. But you know, she's so old and everything . . .' My voice tails off when I realize that there isn't really any excuse. I thought she was old. I thought she hated me. I forgot she was real.

Frog Boy gets to his feet and grabs my hand, pulling me up to a standing position.

'I don't know how to make it better,' I tell him as we start walking back towards the house.

He stops for a moment, pulling his jumper on, and even though the jumper is muffling his face when he speaks, I can still clearly hear his reply.

'We'll think of something,' he says, and as his head pops out of the neck of his jumper he smiles at me reassuringly. 'There's still weeks of the holiday left. We'll work on it together.'

We. Together. Just like that I feel my guilt get less. Like Frog Boy has actually taken some of it from me. I have someone to talk to who can talk back. Someone who will listen and share their thoughts. I am not alone.

I'M TOO SAD TO
TELL YOU*

The human body is a weird thing. Adults go on
and on about healthy eating and doing lots of
exercise but they don't tell you that if you really
want your body to be happy then you have to
keep your head happy too. I'm eating just as
healthily as I was when Mum still lived with us
(in fact I eat way more fruit because it doesn't
have to be cooked, so Dad has given me free rein
of the fruit bowl) and I seem to spend most of my

* *I'm Too Sad to Tell You* (1970) by Bas Jan Ader. This
photograph is a self-portrait. The artist never told anyone
why he was so sad, but he sent this photo to his friends.
Sometimes words don't work. Sometimes we have to find
other ways to tell people how we're feeling. Sometimes
nobody can hear your voice.

time outside at the moment (and fresh air is supposed to be good for you). But my body feels tired and droopy and like it aches all the time. It never used to feel like that.

It aches most when Mum phones me. When I hang up the phone after yet another stilted, difficult conversation, the ache starts in my chest and spreads along my arms and legs until I feel like I can't even climb the stairs to bed. I want to ask her about how I can make the pain go away, but I don't. Because it's all her fault in the first place. She doesn't get to be the solution.

I felt especially tired after Beatrice spoke to me a few days ago. I'd gone to find her to ask if I could have another chance with Martha. We didn't talk about the fall, but she must know that something went wrong. She didn't answer me immediately; instead she stared at me until I thought she must be seeing into my soul, or something. Then she told me that Martha was fragile and needed looking after. She told me about the stroke.

I just can't figure out why it happens. How can getting ill mean that just one side of the body stops working? It makes no sense. Beatrice told me that Martha can't move the right side of her body and she can't talk. That's why she only uses her left hand and writes everything down – and it's why her writing is such a state. She said that it was a terrible thing for a woman like Martha to lose her independence and freedom. I can totally sympathize with how THAT must feel.

But I've been given another chance and I'm determined not to mess up this time. Martha has agreed to meet up with me so we're back in our usual spot and I'm reading aloud from a book that Beatrice has given me. I'm not even sure that it's a book that Martha is enjoying but it's good to have something to do and anything is better than sitting in silence. I'm seeing Frog Boy again later on and I think how good it'll be to tell him I've actually done something. I think he's the kind of person who cares about doing the right thing, so he should be totally impressed that I've given some of my time to cheering Martha up. I never knew that doing good deeds could actually make you feel kind of happy inside. Maybe I've got a talent and I'll spend my life travelling around the world, bestowing happiness and harmony wherever I go. My role models will be Mother Theresa and Florence Nightingale and, and ... erm ... other inspirational women who put the needs of others before their own.

I finish the chapter and stretch out, enjoying the warmth of the sun on my legs. Next to me, I can feel Martha relax in her chair. It's quite nice, sitting here. This week has gone really quickly, between spending the mornings in my hideaway and the afternoons either pretending to garden or with Martha. I can't believe that the holidays are nearly halfway through.

I start wondering about what Lauren and Nat have been up to. I had an email the other day from Nat, asking if my ban had been lifted. She said that Lauren had gone to Cornwall for a week with her parents and that she was bored. And then she told me that they've been planning a barbecue party for next Wednesday and that *surely* my dad will give me the day off – what with it being my *birthday* and everything.

Just remembering this puts me in an instant bad mood. It feels like a cloud has gone in front of the sun but when I look up, the sky is still blue. I sit up straight, feeling fury flooding through me. I've behaved really well for the last few weeks but I'm still going to have the worst birthday ever. It's been Seventy-one Days Without Mum and I still can't get used to the fact that she's on her sunny, happy summer holidays with her new family and won't be there when I wake up in the morning.

'It's so completely unfair,' I mutter. Beside me, Martha lifts her head and looks questioningly at me. 'My parents must really hate me,' I tell her.

Martha frowns and tilts her head to one side, which I take as encouragement to continue.

'It's my birthday next week and my mum is on some stupid holiday with her new, perfect family. She wanted me to go with them – said that she's never been away from me on my birthday before. That's not my fault, is it? And my friends are organizing a party for me and there's no way that Dad will let me go so there's no point in even asking him. I don't see why I'm even bothering to be good, it's not like anybody notices.'

I'm warming up to my theme now and it feels good to be talking about it. 'Dad isn't interested in discussing soppy stuff like feelings and I'm not going to speak to Mum – she doesn't deserve to know how I'm feeling. I might as well have had a stroke like you – except nobody would actually notice if I didn't speak because nobody actually listens to me in the first place.'

Martha jerks her head and her eyebrows squeeze together – I think she's trying to tell me that I'm wrong.

'It's *true*,' I tell her. 'You don't know my parents so you can't understand. They haven't even asked me what I want for my birthday. How heartless is that? I'll probably be lucky to get a card. Maybe Mum will bring me a lame straw donkey back from Spain. Ooh, lucky me.'

I get up and start pacing the ground in front of Martha's wheelchair. 'I've done everything that they've asked of me – right down to spending my holidays in this stupid place.' I look over at Martha. 'No offence.'

She shrugs at me and I imagine her voice in my head, agreeing that Oak Hill is indeed a stupid place. I don't think Martha wants to be here any more than I do.

'I never get anything that I actually want,' I tell her. 'Not even when it's free and wouldn't cost them a penny.'

I slump back on to the bench and Martha slowly uses her left hand to turn her chair so that she's right next to me. She pats my knee and I look up into her face. The young Martha's eyes are gazing at me and if I ignore the wrinkly skin then I could be talking to one of my friends. And actually, it's so nice to have someone actually listening to me without constantly interrupting that I don't care about the wrinkles and the loose skin over her cheekbones.

?

scrawls Martha on her notepad. And if it was anyone else I wouldn't say, but the fact that she won't repeat my secrets and the way that she's looking at me as if she really cares, makes me suddenly long to say the words.

I look into her eyes and everything just comes tumbling out of my mouth.

'I just want my mum and dad back together again. I want to be a family – the three of us and Picasso, my dog. I want to wake up on Saturday mornings and smell Mum making waffles for breakfast. I want to go to sleep listening to the sounds of the television while Mum and Dad watch a film. I want to have them both come to watch my school concert on the same night, not planning it to make sure they don't meet up. I want Dad to smile again and Mum to tell me off for not washing up my cereal bowl after breakfast.'

I stop, partly because I'm out of breath and partly because I can feel tears prickling in the backs of my eyes. I didn't even know that I was bothered about some of this stuff.

Martha is waiting, watching my face.

'I want us all to live happily ever after,' I whisper, so quietly that I can barely hear myself, and as I speak the words I know that they are true. I'm not stupid – I know that life doesn't always turn out the way you want it to. I just didn't know that my family would end up like this – spoilt and a bit rubbish. Like the shininess has rubbed off.

Martha picks up her notepad, a frown on her face. It's a long message and it takes her a minute or so to write the words with her left hand. When she's done she rips the page out and thrusts it across to where I'm sitting on the bench. I read it and then it's my turn to frown.

FORGET HAPPY ENDINGS. BETTER TO LOOK FOR A NEW BEGINNING

I think about what she's written. Forget happy endings? How am I supposed to do that? I mean, I know that 'happy ever after' doesn't always work out, but surely I can hope that *some* things will end up OK? If Martha thinks that I should just accept my rubbish life then she doesn't know me very well.

'Are you telling me that I should just give up?' I ask her, my voice betraying how hurt I feel.

I should have known better than to think that she would understand.

Martha shakes her head.

'Then what *are* you saying?' I'm trying not to sound cross but it's so frustrating. I just want her to tell me. I can't be bothered to second-guess what she's thinking. I read the note again and feel anger rising in me.

'Forget happy endings? That's not a very grown-up thing to say, is it? And I should just look for a new beginning? How does that help? That's exactly what Mum's done but it isn't a new beginning for me, is it? Or Dad. We're left with the old, miserable ending while she starts again with a brand new *once upon a time*. I don't want a new beginning! I want my old story back.'

I stand up, stuffing the note in my pocket. Martha is looking at me and I can see that she's upset – her left arm is reaching out for me and her right hand is jerking free of the blanket that tucks it by her side. I need to leave; she can't help me right now if she hasn't got words to make it better.

But I can't go. I can't make the same mistake twice. I've been given a second chance to start afresh with Martha, I can't get it wrong again. Mother Theresa wouldn't walk away right now. I sink back on to the bench and stare at the water fountain, Martha's words rolling around my brain. I think about Dad and how unhappy he's been. It'd be much better for him if he could have a new beginning. But how many times are you allowed to start again? You can't just keep on reinventing your life every time it doesn't go the way you want it to.

'Surely you have to commit to seeing something through to the end eventually?' I mutter. 'Everyone must get to have at least one happy ending?'

Martha makes a small noise in her throat and I look over at her. She hunches one shoulder in a kind of half-shrug and looks down at herself, her eyebrows raised. Then she does her weird smile and nods at me, and her eyes are telling me things that she can't say with words.

And I sort of get it. Maybe it's OK to look for as many new beginnings as you need to, because when the end finally arrives, when your time is up and you're old and tired, there is absolutely no stopping it. Although I'm not sure that it can accurately be called a *happy* ending. There's nothing happy about being ancient, is there?

New beginnings. I suppose it isn't the worst idea I've ever heard. Beginnings sound a lot more exciting than endings, that's for sure. Less final.

I reach across for Martha's hand at the same time that she reaches for mine and we sit together until Beatrice comes back. When Martha has gone I miss the feel of her hand holding mine and making me feel like there's at least one person in the world who understands.

MARTHA

When I was a girl I spent hours planning my life. How I would marry Tommy and we would have two children – one boy and one girl. We would live in a cottage in the country and grow vegetables and I would collect eggs from our own chickens. I would grow old with Tommy beside me.

Those hours were a waste of time. Happy endings only happen in fairy stories. Real life is about starting over, again and again, and hoping each time that maybe this will be the fresh beginning you were waiting for.

But I am a hypocrite. It is not a fresh beginning if you continue to make the same mistakes. I left Tommy in the woods that day when we were children and three years later I would do it again, all the time believing that I was searching out a new beginning.

It was the spring of 1945 and I was sixteen years old. Tommy and I had been courting for three years and I thought we had a whole lifetime ahead of us. He had already secretly proposed to me and I had accepted. We decided not to tell our parents until he turned eighteen in the autumn of that year but there was no doubt in my mind that Tommy was the love of my life and that I was the love of his. He bought me a wedding ring (I'm not sure how he got his hands on it and I thought it best not to ask) and it was tucked away at the bottom of my gas-mask box, ready for the day I would wear it with pride.

I remember that I had packed a picnic. It was Tommy's suggestion that we cycle out to the woods and it was a warm day for early April. I was wearing a dress that I had made out of an old pair of curtains. We used to do that kind of thing back then. We saw possibility and opportunity in everything. I was very fond of that dress – I thought the cut of the material showed off my slim waist rather well. It wasn't the most practical item of clothing for a cycle ride but I was far too vain to worry about tiny details like that.

The woods were beautiful. I'd packed a picnic rug and when I threw it on to the ground it all seemed so perfect. My hair was auburn in those days and the sunlight streaming through the branches caught the red highlights and made me look like a film star. So I told myself, anyway. Tommy settled himself down next to me and I was just reaching for the picnic hamper when he ruined it all.

It was his duty, he told me. He was needed on the front and it was his duty to go. I laughed at first and told him that there would be plenty of time for fighting when he was a man. I wasn't particularly worried. The war made life difficult but other than the occasional nightmare about my German pilot I hadn't felt its effect on my life. Not really. This was a war about other people, not Tommy and I.

I stopped laughing when Tommy stood up. He had a quiet determination about him that day that I had not seen before and it made me uneasy. I told him to sit back down and stop being a fool and did he want a ham roll? 'I'm going,' he said to me. 'I'm going to help win this war.'

I started to feel angry then. Looking back now I can tell that I was scared but at the time I just felt cross. He'd never be allowed to fight without his parents' permission, I told him. And his mother would rather fight the Nazis with her rolling pin than let him out of her sight. That was when he told me his plan. He was leaving today. Our trip to the woods was a goodbye picnic. He would lie about his age, he said, and I knew they'd believe him. Tommy was strong and broad but he was just a boy. A boy who had no right to be fighting with grown men.

I stood up too and faced him. 'Don't do this,' I told him. He tried to take my hand but I snatched it away. 'If you leave now then you leave me,' I said. 'I won't wait for you while you go off to be killed.'

The look on his face nearly broke me but I meant every word. And I thought it would be enough to make him stay. But it was not.

'I promise I'll come home,' he told me but I had heard enough. Abandoning the picnic rug and hamper I stormed out of the wood and across the field to where we had left our bicycles. I turned just once and saw Tommy standing beneath the trees at the edge of the wood. He raised his hand at me and waved but I ignored him. I left him there, all alone, and the whole way home I told myself that I was doing the right thing. That I refused to be made a war widow before I was even married.

Tommy broke his promise but it wasn't really his fault. I don't blame him anyway. He didn't even make it as far as the front line. They said the bomb killed him instantly, as if there was supposed to be some comfort in that fact. For myself, I would have preferred to know that he had one last moment of knowing. Knowing that he had been; that he had happened.

Those children that I dreamt of never arrived but if they had I wouldn't have read them bedtime stories of *happily ever after*. I would have told them that if they couldn't find a happy ending, then they needed to put in some effort and search for a new beginning. As many times as necessary. Because you have to write your own story and it might not be a fairy tale.

THE PERSISTENCE
OF MEMORY*

I've decided to introduce Frog Boy to Martha.
After all, if he's going to help me come up with a
solution to the Martha Problem then he needs to
know what we're dealing with and he told me
that he's never really met her properly, apart from
that horrible day when she fell out of her wheelchair

* *The Persistence of Memory* (1931) by Salvador Dali.
This painting shows three watches that have all melted
and are oozing over various things. They have all stopped
at different times, which is why I *think* it's called *The
Persistence Of Memory*. No matter how much time passes
and no matter what terrible things may happen, we still
remember. Sometimes I'm glad to have memories and
sometimes I wish that they'd go away. Memories aren't
always a good thing – not if they remind you of something
you'll never have ever again.

and he came to the rescue. I ask Beatrice to bring Martha to the water fountain in the afternoon and we're waiting for her, sitting side by side on the bench when she arrives.

Beatrice leaves and we sit in silence until I realize that it's probably my responsibility to do the talking.

'Er – so, this is Martha,' I say, gesturing towards Martha where she is sitting in her wheelchair with an amused expression on her face. 'And . . . er . . . this is Fro–' I stop, mid-word, horrified with myself.

Frog Boy looks at me quizzically.

'What were you about to call me?' he asks.

'Nothing!' I say, my voice sounding squeaky.

'Yes, you were,' he says. 'You were introducing me and you said "This is fro–' What's "fro"?'

'You misheard,' I mutter. 'I was telling Martha that your name is –'

I stop again and close my eyes, wishing that I could start this all over again. I am not doing well.

'My name is . . .?' questions Frog Boy. He's not going to let this go. 'Oh, wow! You can't actually remember my name, can you?'

I open my eyes and look at him with the best apologetic look I can muster.

'I am SO sorry. I couldn't remember it after we first met, and it hasn't come up since. And then I forgot that I didn't know.'

'So what have you been calling me, then? You know – in your mind,' he asks. I look at him and try to feign confusion, but I know exactly what he means. We've spent hours together – he knows that I must have been referring to him as *something* in my head.

'Er . . .' I say intelligently, looking at Martha and hoping that maybe she'll do something amazing and distract him from this topic of conversation. No luck there, though – she looks like she's thoroughly enjoying every moment of my discomfort and has absolutely no intention of breaking up the entertainment.

'I've been calling you Frog Boy in my head,' I say miserably, mentally waving goodbye to a beautiful friendship that will now be over before it even began.

'Frog Boy?' He sounds confused. 'Why would you call me that?'

'You know. The frog. The weird, warty one that you thought was so fascinating, the day we met. I thought you must have a thing about frogs, so I called you Frog Boy . . .' I tail off, sounding pathetic.

He looks at me, utterly bewildered for a moment, until suddenly a short laugh bursts out of his mouth. It's followed by another, longer laugh and it's so infectious that Martha joins in. Her laugh is totally silent but her body is shaking and her eyes look happy. I'd join in too if I wasn't feeling so awful.

Eventually they calm down and he turns to me.

'But, Erin, it wasn't even a frog!' he says, and bursts out laughing again. 'It was a toad,' he splutters, leaning across the bench and grasping Martha's shoulder for support as laughter wracks his body, making him shake.

'All right, whatever,' I say, feeling a bit grumpy. It's not that funny, or if it is then I don't get the joke. 'Toad, frog – they're all the same thing.'

'No, they're not,' he tells me, sitting up straight and obviously trying to get a grip. 'But the point is, you should have been calling me Toad Boy all along!' This starts him off again and I look away in disgust. I'm glad he isn't upset but we've got serious business to get down to here, and I don't like being laughed at.

'Anyway,' he says to Martha, taking a deep breath. 'Let me introduce myself to you. My name is Frog Boy and I'm very pleased to meet you!' He holds out his left hand towards Martha's left hand and she shakes it, her eyes dancing and her mouth grinning widely. She obviously thinks he's completely fantastic, which is good – as long as they don't both forget who introduced them in the first place.

'I'm sorry,' I say to him. 'What IS your name?'

Frog Boy leans back on the bench. 'Frog Boy,' he tells me.

'No! Seriously. Just tell me and we can forget about this whole, stupid conversation.'

He grins at me, a wicked grin that makes me feel a bit nervous. 'I think Frog Boy really suits me. You can always call me Frog for short, if you feel it's a bit of a mouthful.'

'Fine,' I say, shrugging my shoulders and looking past him to where Martha is sitting. 'Just remember this is your choice.'

'Absolutely,' he says firmly.

'And I think you're completely weird,' I add.

'Undoubtedly,' agrees Frog.

'Fine, then,' I say.

'Yes, it is,' he says, nodding at me.

I have lost any control of this ridiculous situation and feel the need to change the topic of conversation as quickly as possible.

'So, what shall we talk about?' I say breezily, while mentally kicking myself. *What shall we talk about?* How is that ever going to be a conversation starter?

'Er . . . I don't know,' says Frog. 'What do you normally talk about?'

That is a good question. What *do* we usually talk about? What did we talk about yesterday? Oh yeah – I had a mental moment at Martha. I feel myself going red at the memory but fortunately, Martha has written a note.

DANCING

Unfortunately, she has chosen my least favourite topic of conversation.

'We do *not* normally talk about dancing!' I tell her.

'I don't mind if that's what you like talking about, Erin,' says Frog, grinning at me.

'I *don't*!' My voice comes out in a squeal and I take a deep breath, trying to get it under control.

'I quite like dancing,' he continues. 'As long as nobody is actually watching!'

'Yes, well, I don't,' I state. 'Now someone suggest a sensible topic of conversation.'

Cue another note from Martha.

JITTERBUG

I groan. 'Martha, we are so not talking about dancing. If that's what jitterbug even means. Sounds like some weird kind of insect to me.'

'You aren't very cultured, are you?' says Frog and I elbow him in the ribs.

'And I suppose you are?' I ask him as he doubles up dramatically, clutching his side.

'I'm cultured enough to know that the jitterbug was this type of crazy dance people used to do in the nineteen forties and nineteen fifties. Am I right?'

He looks at Martha, who nods and smiles. Encouraged, Frog keeps talking. 'It's really energetic, lots of swinging around and jumping and moving your feet really quickly.'

'Well, I can tell you right now that I would be terrible at it,' I say. 'I do not have any dancing ability whatsoever. In fact, I have this recurring nightmare where I'm dancing on a stage and everyone is watching me and pointing and laughing.'

'Do you have any clothes on?' sniggers Frog and I round on him.

'What sort of a question is that? Yes, I have clothes on. Jeez – what is with you today?' I huff and turn to Martha. 'Anyway, as I was saying, in my dream I –'

I am rudely interrupted by another note, which is thrust in front of my face.

NOBODY CARES IF YOU CAN'T DANCE WELL – JUST GET UP AND DANCE!

'Yes, well, thanks for the motivational quote. It's easy for you to say,' I start, and then I realize what I've said. 'Oh no, I didn't mean it was easy like that; I mean, I know you can't dance now or anything and . . .' I trail off. I am just making it worse. I need to shut my big, fat gob before I do any more damage. Or create a diversion, maybe.

'So,' I say, 'anyone fancy taking my dad's van for a spin?'

There is silence, only broken after a few humiliating moments by the sound of Frog swallowing loudly.

'Did you dance the jitterbug, Martha?' Frog isn't looking at me so the weapons of mass destruction that I am firing out of my eyes miss him by a mile. It's kind of hard to imagine Martha dancing, when her legs obviously don't work.

I tense, waiting for Martha to get upset, but she surprises me, though – she sits up straight and nods.

'Do you miss dancing?' asks Frog quietly. I glare at him – that's kind of an insensitive thing to say to someone who will never dance again. And can't he tell that I'm trying to change the subject? But Martha turns her head, stares hard at him and smiles a sad little smile, before sinking into her wheelchair and lowering her head so that her chin droops down on to her chest.

I elbow Frog in the ribs. 'Maybe you'll be able to dance again, one day,' I tell Martha. 'If you work on your exercises. Those ones that Beatrice is always telling you to do.' Frog frowns and opens his mouth to speak but I don't want him doing any more damage so I interrupt him. 'You could show us how you used to do that dance. The jitterbug, wasn't it? I'd love to see that.'

I'm keen to cheer Martha up by any means possible, even if it does mean telling the odd little white lie.

I rattle on for a few more minutes, with Martha ignoring me, and Frog watching us both, with a funny expression on his face. It's a relief when Beatrice walks round the corner to take Martha back to the house. I am not skilled at social chit-chat.

I round on Frog the second that Beatrice disappears along the path.

'What did you say that for, you big idiot?' I ask him. I'm really cross. I wanted him and Martha to get along and everything was going fine until he opened his huge mouth and upset her.

'What's the problem?' he asks.

'You're the problem, dumb-head,' I say. 'Asking Martha if she misses dancing.'

'It was just a question,' he says, and I sigh, wondering if all boys are this insensitive.

'Yes,' I tell him. 'But all that talk of dancing made her realize that her dancing days are over. How upsetting is *that* for poor Martha?'

Frog looks at me like I'm being a bit stupid and I resist the urge to punch him on the leg.

'Erin,' he says slowly. 'I think Martha knows that she won't be doing the jitterbug again, don't you?'

'But it doesn't hurt to tell her that she might, does it?' I explode at him. 'You know – give her something to look forward to. A bit of hope.'

'I think you're wrong,' says Frog, standing up and walking over to the fountain. 'I think lying to her is patronizing. She's not a child. She knows what she can and can't do. I think Martha would prefer people to be honest with her.'

'Oh, and you're basing this on knowing her for all of five seconds, are you?' I'm properly angry now. How dare he waltz in here and act like he knows Martha better than I do. She's MY friend.

OK, yes – she IS. She's actually my friend. I've told her stuff I haven't told anyone else and I'm the one who can help her to get better.

'You can't help her get better from being old,' Frog tells me, once again behaving like a freaky mind reader. 'And the reason I asked if she missed dancing was because I thought we could figure out a way to show her some jitterbug dancing. Like on YouTube, or something.'

'Oh.' I am quiet for a moment, letting this new information sink in. 'I suppose that *is* quite a good idea.' I know that my voice sounds grudging but I'm a bit fed up that I didn't think of it myself.

'I know you want to help Martha,' says Frog, coming back to sit next to me on the bench. 'And so do I. But I don't think you have to pretend that she's going to suddenly leap out of her wheelchair and start racing round the garden. I think she just likes having a bit of company.'

I look at the water fountain. The water has gone – it's completely dry because of the baking hot sun.

'I don't even know why she mentioned dancing in the first place,' I grumble. 'Not if it was just going to make her all miserable and depressed.'

Frog picks up a pebble and throws it towards the fountain. It falls into the lowest basin with a clattering sound.

'I think she likes remembering. Memories are probably a bit pointless if you've got nobody to share them with.'

I choose a pebble and aim it carefully.

'Ten points if I get this in the top basin,' I say, but my throw goes wide and the pebble shoots off into a bush. 'That was a practice shot,' I inform Frog, bending down and choosing another pebble.

'So you reckon it'll cheer Martha up if we show her some clips of people dancing the jitterbug?'

This time my pebble flies through the air beautifully, curving down towards the water fountain and falling into the top basin with a satisfying thud.

'Well, it's probably not as good as watching it for real, but we can try,' says Frog.

'What is the jitterbug, anyway?' I ask him.

'I'm not totally sure,' he admits. 'But I do know it's kind of fast and a bit tricky. I'll Google it when I get home later and see what I can find out. I'll be back here on Thursday. Meet you then?'

I nod and feel glad that we've got some sort of a plan. But I know, deep down, that Frog has got it wrong. I CAN help Martha get better. I can help her have a better life, maybe even a longer life – that's why she likes hanging out with me. I'm doing something worthwhile, something that shows I can be a good, inspirational sort of person after all, no matter what Mum thinks about me.

SUMMER *

I wake up on the morning of my thirteenth birthday feeling miserable. Seventy-six Days Without Mum and I'm fairly sure today is going to be rubbish. Dad has never been responsible for my birthday before. It always used to be Mum who planned my parties and bought my presents. Dad would write his name in the card.

I get up as slowly as possible and throw on the same clothes that I wore yesterday. I can't be bothered to make an effort, specially as Frog isn't going to Oak Hill today. I've turned off my phone

* *Summer* (1573) by Giuseppe Arcimboldo. This is cool! I'm definitely going to try to do this myself – make my own face using fruit and vegetables. I really like his cucumber nose and his peapod smile. I bet Giuseppe was a fun person to hang around with. And let's face it – it's way more exciting to create art with this stuff than to actually eat it!

and I'm avoiding the computer. I'm not sure I could cope with hearing all about Lauren and Nat's amazing plans for their barbecue party. I didn't bother asking Dad if I could have the day off from my punishment. I know that stealing his money was a really bad thing to do. I suppose I'm lucky that he hasn't spent the entire summer sulking with me.

The first surprise of the day happens as I'm brushing my hair. The sound of four feet bounding up the stairs and into my room is so unexpected that I hardly have time to turn round before Picasso throws himself at me and I stagger back on to the bed. For a little dog he can be very energetic sometimes – although I haven't seen him behave like this for ages.

'What are *you* doing up here?' I gasp, grabbing hold of his long body and burying my face in his neck, smelling his lovely Picasso smell. He replies by giving me a huge, sloppy lick, which makes me squeal. Then he flops down on to the bed next to me, panting and looking at me with his huge brown and blue eyes.

Picasso is NOT allowed in my bedroom. In fact, he's not allowed upstairs, full stop. This was one of the things that Mum and Dad were in perfect agreement about. Picasso always knows that he'll be in serious trouble if even one paw touches the first stair. That means that one of two things has just happened. Either Dad let him come up to me or Picasso knows it's my birthday and is risking a telling-off so that he can be with me.

'At least *someone* knows today is an important day,' I tell him, ruffling the fur behind his ears, just how he likes it.

I spend ten minutes cuddling Picasso and trying not to remember this time last year, when Mum and Dad took me to London for my twelfth birthday treat and everything was good and my family was a proper family. Then I hear Dad clattering about downstairs and realize that if I want to start the day with breakfast then I need to move.

Picasso and I slink out of my bedroom door and across the landing. Picasso is an excellent slinker – he was born to slink. I look at him and put my finger to my lips, and then, keeping my back pressed against the wall, put my foot on the top stair. The theme tune from *Mission Impossible* is in my head and I bend down, putting one hand on Picasso's collar so I can guide him slowly towards the hall.

Just as we're halfway down, the kitchen door opens and Dad comes out. We freeze, me with one foot in mid-air and Picasso stretched across three stairs. But Dad goes into the living room and I take my chance, launching myself down the remaining stairs with my daft dog flinging himself after me. We race down the hall and into the kitchen and by the time Dad comes back in I am sitting at the kitchen table.

Dad glances at Picasso, who is trying to look casual, but completely overdoing it. He is flopped in his basket with his tail wagging madly and as Dad looks at him he seems to raise one eyebrow, as if he's saying *What? I haven't done anything!* I glare at him behind Dad's back and I swear he grins at me. That, or I really need to spend more time with actual people this summer.

Dad smiles at Picasso and then walks over to the kitchen counter.

'I've made you some toast,' he says, handing me a plate. 'Happy Birthday, lovely girl!'

'Thanks, Dad!' This is the second surprise of the day, and it's only 8 a.m.

The third surprise is only moments behind the second. Dad sits down opposite me and starts buttering his own toast.

'You don't need to come in with me today,' he tells me. I'm so busy watching, transfixed, as he spreads half a pot of strawberry jam on one piece of toast that it takes a few moments for his words to sink in.

'What?' I ask him. 'Why?' Obviously, turning thirteen hasn't improved my ability to speak elegantly.

'You've been really good about going to Oak Hill every day,' he says. I have no idea how he's going to eat that toast without spreading it over half his face. It's literally dripping with jam. 'You deserve the day off. And I gather your friends have plans for you. They can be very persuasive when they want something – quite terrifying, actually.' He grins at me and raises an eyebrow.

I look at him in shock. I didn't say a word about the barbecue party, which means that Lauren and Nat must have told him. And he's actually letting me go? It's quite possible that my friends are the best friends in the entire universe.

Quickly I turn my head to look out of the window. Today can't really be this good – it must be pouring with rain or thunder and lightning. But no – the sky is a brilliant blue and the sun is already shining brightly. Perfect weather for a barbecue.

I look back at Dad. The toast has been eaten in three bites and none of it is on his face. Impressive.

'Thanks, Dad,' I say. He nods at me and gets up to rinse his plate under the tap. The standard of washing-up in this house has definitely deteriorated since Mum left.

'Really. Thank you,' I repeat, wanting him to know how much I appreciate this. He hasn't given me a gift or anything but at least he hasn't forgotten. And he's giving me a whole day with my friends, which is kind of like a present.

Dad walks over to me and I stand up. He pulls me into a big hug that lasts for a while and when it ends he lets go of me and takes a step back, looking at me hard.

'We're OK, aren't we?' he asks me. He sounds nervous and I suddenly have a flash of insight about what this might all be like for him. Looking after a teenage girl on his own probably wasn't his idea of living happily ever after. When him and Mum got married he probably thought it would last forever. And I know that he didn't want her to leave. I heard him telling her, one awful night, that he'd always love her, no matter what. And that if she ever changed her mind then he'd be here, waiting for her.

'We're fine, Dad,' I tell him. I've been a selfish cow. I'm not saying he's the best father in the world, but he's the one I've got and at least he's here with me. Not off with another family, trying to find perfection in a new beginning.

'I know this isn't like your other birthdays,' he says quietly. 'Everything's different to how it was before.' I have never heard my dad sound so unsure. It makes me stand up a bit taller.

'Different is OK,' I tell him. 'We're starting again, you and me. It doesn't have to be the same as it used to be.'

Dad smiles at me. 'When did you get so old and wise?' he jokes.

'Oh, about thirty seconds ago,' I say. 'I AM thirteen now, you know.'

'Don't I know it.' He looks at me again. 'You're growing up, Erin. If you'd rather live with Mum for a while then I'd understand.'

My eyes flash towards Picasso, who has sat up since this conversation began, looking eagerly between us as if he understands every word that we're saying.

'Mum has agreed that Picasso can live at her house, if that's where you want to be,' says Dad, sounding as if he is making himself tell me this new piece of information.

I pause, thinking carefully. I've missed Mum so much over the last few weeks, even if I am furious with her. But sometimes it's a mistake to try and hold on to the past.

'She's really not coming home, is she?' I ask Dad. He shakes his head sadly but firmly.

'Then it's time for a new beginning,' I tell him. 'Me and you and Picasso. Boldly going where no family has gone before. Well, actually, they probably have, but we haven't so it's a whole new beginning for us.' I stop, before my rambling gets any worse.

'A whole new beginning,' repeats Dad. 'Yes, I like the sound of that.' He looks out of the window and smiles to himself, before turning back to me. 'Have a great day, sweetheart. And enjoy the first day of being a real-life teenager!'

'Thanks, Dad,' I say. Maybe this day will turn out to be better than I expected.

After Dad leaves for Oak Hill I wash up my plate and cup and head back upstairs. When I walk into my bedroom, the fourth surprise of the day is waiting for me. There, lying on my bed, is a parcel. It's sort of square and quite flat and looks like something that I might really, really want to have.

Stuck to the top is a gift label. Tearing it off I turn it over and read the message.

To Erin. Happy Birthday. Mum and I both agreed that this would be the right time for you to have this. Love Dad x

I sit down on my bed and pick up the parcel. Its weight is familiar and with my heart pounding I pull off the wrapping paper and look at the plain white box. It's beautiful and even before I open it up I know exactly what's inside. I just can't quite bring myself to believe that they've let me have it, after everything that's happened.

My hands are shaking as I open the lid. And there it is. My own iPad. I pull it out and look at the back, just to be sure. *Erin Edwards* is engraved on to the metal.

I turn it on eagerly and spend the next twenty minutes playing around. It takes me no time to get my email set up and when I check my inbox I see that Lauren and Nat have both sent me messages, telling me that the barbecue party starts at 3 p.m. and I'd better not be late. Lauren has sent me an extra, shorter message telling me to wear my funkiest clothes and put some make-up on. I ignore her – I am totally not putting on make-up for a barbecue with my two best friends! It's not like there'll be anybody there who needs impressing.

I grab my iPad and go back downstairs. Picasso is waiting for me in the hall and I decide that, as it IS my birthday, he should be allowed in the living room with me. After all, it was mostly Mum who had a problem with him. She made a house rule that he was only allowed in the hall and the kitchen because she 'didn't want dog hair all over the cushions and beds'. Dad probably only went along with it to make her happy. I'm starting to think he did quite a lot of that.

I sink down on to the sofa with Picasso snuggled up next to me and carry on playing with my iPad. It's when I'm on level five of Angry Birds that I realize something is wrong.

I put down the iPad and stroke Picasso, trying to work out why I'm feeling weird. There's a churning sensation in my stomach and my head feels crowded – like there's a thought trying to push its way in but I'm not letting it. I get up and stretch. Maybe a drink and a biscuit will sort me out. Picasso's asleep again so I cover him with the blanket off the back of the sofa (Mum would literally have a fit if she could see me doing this) and walk into the kitchen. I put the kettle on and while I'm waiting for it to boil I hear the thunk of the post dropping through our letterbox.

Racing into the hall I see a huge pile of brightly coloured envelopes and a slightly squashed Jiffy bag lying on the doormat. I recognize Mum's writing on the squashed parcel immediately so I open it up and pull out a postcard with a picture of a donkey on the front. Mum's written to me on the back:

Dear Erin,

Happy 13th Birthday! I so wish that I could be with you today but I bet you're having a great time with your friends! Maybe you'd like to come over when we get back from holidays and we can celebrate your birthday all over again?

*Do you like the picture on this postcard? I chose
it because the place we're staying has a donkey
that looks just like this one! The boys have been
having such fun, feeding him carrots and going for
rides. I wish you were here with us - I think you'd
love it.*

*Have a great day! I can't believe my little girl is
13 years old! I can't wait to see you. Mark and the
boys send their love.*

*Lots of love,
Mum*

*PS The enclosed is just a daft little extra present!
Your real present from Dad and me is the iPad.*

I put my hand inside the Jiffy bag and feel something hard. Pulling it out, I unfold it to see that Mum has sent me a Spanish fan. It's completely not me – as if I've got any use for an old-lady fan. Though I suppose I should be grateful that it isn't a straw donkey.

Back in the living room I walk over to the sofa. Picasso is still snuggled up like a baby under his blanket, fast asleep and snoring quietly – funny little dog snores that make me smile. I pick up my iPad and settle down next to him. And straight away I feel horrible again, like my insides are squirming with snakes. I can feel the awful thought, battering against my brain and demanding to be let in, and this time I can't keep it away. I know exactly why I'm feeling like this.

I feel guilty.

I look down at the iPad in my hands and I know that I totally don't deserve to have it. In an absolute, definite, I-am-not-good-enough kind of way.

I stole from my dad. The same dad who has always been there for me even when I've behaved like a brat. Even when he's been so sad that he seems to have forgotten how to smile. And Mum. She's tried pretty hard to talk to me about everything but I've completely ignored her. I even pretended I couldn't hear her when she last tried to talk to me about why her and Dad have split up.

I've been so angry with Mum and Dad for the last few months and I've sort of got used to feeling mad at them most of the time. But I don't feel angry now. This is much worse. I wish they'd never let me have this stupid iPad back because now it feels like I'm the bad one. Which I suppose I am, in a way.

I turn off the iPad and carefully pack it back into the box. Then I put it high up on a shelf above the TV. It'll be safe there and maybe I'll start to feel a bit better if I'm not actually looking at it.

I spend the rest of the morning tidying my room and reading my book. Weirdly, I keep thinking about Oak Hill and what Martha's doing. I know Frog isn't visiting his grandad today but even so, I can't stop thinking about what I'd be doing if I were there. When lunchtime comes I make a cheese sandwich but it doesn't taste as good as it normally does when I'm sitting with Dad in the garden, my back propped up against his shed and the sun on my face.

I'm glad when 2.30 p.m. finally arrives and I can get ready to go out. I'm already dressed in jeans and a T-shirt and anything else would seem silly for a barbecue, so I give my hair a quick brush and grab my hoody. Then I put Picasso's lead on him and together we walk over to Nat's house.

By the time we get there it's 3.10 p.m. I can hear voices coming from the back garden and so

I ignore the front door and head down the path at the side of the house. Pushing open the wooden gate I step on to the lawn. And stand very still.

Nat's garden is heaving with people. I recognize most of them from school but they're not people that we'd normally hang out with. For a split second I think I've got the wrong house by mistake and I'm just about to turn and drag Picasso away before we're spotted when a voice yells my name.

'Erin! You made it!'

I squint into the crowd of people standing on the patio, and as faces turn to look in my direction I see Nat shoving her way through and then running across the lawn towards me. I raise my hand in a greeting but to my surprise she grabs me in a hug and then air-kisses each side of my face.

'Happy birthday! I'm so glad you're here!' she squeals. 'We all thought you'd been abducted by aliens! LOZ! Guess who's here! It's Erin!'

This last bit is shrieked at high volume, so now everyone is aware of the fact that I, Erin Edwards, am in the garden. But who on earth is Loz, and why would they be interested in my arrival? I look over at the house to see Lauren, my other best friend, tottering down the steps and across the grass in an insane pair of high heels.

I laugh, starting to feel relaxed. It's so good to see my friends, even if they are acting even crazier than normal. I take in Nat's short, sticky-out skirt and glittery purple eyeshadow, and Lauren's cut-off shorts that would look a bit much even with trainers, never mind heels, and think I'm starting to understand what's going on here.

'Guys! You never told me it was fancy dress!' I whisper to them, glancing around at everyone else. Nobody looks like they're here for a barbecue. Goodness knows how they're going to manage when we start having a water fight or kicking a ball around.

Lauren turns to Nat with a questioning look on her face, but Nat just shrugs her shoulders back at her.

'And who ARE these people? Have they gatecrashed or something?' I ask them. 'Don't you think you should get your parents to tell them to leave?'

Nat bursts out laughing. 'Oh, Erin, I've missed your sense of humour so much! Thank god your dad has finally seen sense and let you have a life!'

I'm not sure what to think when she says this, but before I can say anything Lauren comes and stands right next to me.

'I thought I told you to make an effort with your clothes and stuff,' she whisper-hisses into my ear.

I turn to her and grin. 'Yeah, but if you'd told me it was fancy dress I'd have known what you were going on about, wouldn't I?' I tell her.

Lauren shakes her head. 'It's not fancy dress, Erin,' she says, sounding frustrated. 'Stop saying that. You're going to make yourself sound really dumb in a minute.'

I'm trying really hard to keep up with what's going on here, but my brain just can't figure it out. Lauren obviously thinks I'm being deliberately stupid, but I'm really not. I'm obviously just actually genuinely stupid, because for the life of me I cannot work out why all these random people are standing in my best friend's garden and why everyone except me and Picasso is dressed like they're going clubbing.

'So why are all these people here?' I ask slowly. Nat bursts out laughing again.

'Because they're our friends, of course,' she says.

I must look confused because Lauren scowls at me. She doesn't think I'm being hilarious, which would be reassuring if it wasn't for the fact that I can tell she's getting cross with me.

'You've not been around,' she tells me. 'There's been loads going on this summer. Haven't you been looking at Facebook?' I shake my head, not wanting to tell her that it hurt too much, knowing that they were all getting on with fun stuff without me. 'Well, we've been going to Youth Club and we've met loads of cool people. Some of them are sixteen and they get us drink from the supermarket!'

'Proper drinks, not cola,' adds Nat helpfully. 'You know, with alcohol in it.'

'Great,' I say weakly. Except I'm not sure that it is. 'So what's with the clothes? Are you going out after the barbecue?'

'No,' snaps Lauren. 'This is what *normal* people wear, Erin. You know, if they want to not look like a geek.'

'Oh,' I reply. 'So are you saying that I look like a geek because I'm in jeans and a T-shirt?'

'Yes, but don't worry,' says Nat. 'We're here to help! I've got loads of new stuff in my room and we'll get you looking gorgeous in no time!'

'Oh, I don't . . .' I start, but Nat has grabbed Picasso's lead from my hand and is crouched on the floor, tickling his tummy and making silly baby noises at him.

'Loz – take her upstairs and get started. I'll be with you in a minute,' she tells Lauren.

'I need to get some water for Picasso,' I say feebly.

'I'll do it,' says Nat, stroking his back with long, firm strokes. Like the traitor he is, Picasso stretches out even more than his normal, extraordinarily long self and makes a sound that's almost like a purr. Sometimes I swear that he thinks he's actually a cat. He's unusual like that. Dachshunds are supposed to be suspicious of anyone who isn't their owner, but Picasso is just too daft to be wary of anyone.

Before I can protest, Lauren has put her arm round my shoulder and is leading me towards the throng of people milling about in Nat's garden. We push our way through, Lauren greeting people every two seconds while I look around in the pathetic hope that there might be somebody there who I know to say hello to. But there isn't. I think I see a boy from my maths class, but I've never spoken to him in my life before, so it's not like I can just start up a conversation with him now.

Anyway, Lauren is obviously keen to get me inside before my fashion crime is noticed. She opens the back door and we step through into the kitchen. It's quiet in here and I relax, realizing that I'd been holding my breath as we walked through the garden.

But there's no time for chilling out and chatting. Lauren marches across the kitchen and into the hall.

'Come *on*,' she says to me. 'We've got work to do.'

I follow her upstairs and into Nat's room. It looks different from the last time I was in here and I look around, trying to work out what has changed. The first thing I see is a huge poster above her bed. I burst out laughing.

'Since when has Nat been into *them*?' I ask Lauren. The poster shows five members of a boy band, posing and looking at the camera as if they are in love with it. The hair-gel brigade, we used to call them.

'Duh – since *everyone* was into them,' says Lauren, opening the wardrobe door and pulling out several hangers with clothes draped on to them. Her voice makes it clear that I'm saying something she thinks is stupid. Again. I decide to stop talking.

That lasts about ten seconds, though, because I think of something I really, really want to ask her.

'Lauren,' I say, trying to sound casual.

'Yeah?' The clothes she has piled up in her arms muffle her voice.

'What's with the whole "Loz" thing?' I ask.

She flings the clothes on to the bed and looks at me.

'It's my name,' she says, sounding a bit defensive.

'But we've never called you that before,' I say. I know this is probably dangerous ground, because I can see Lauren's cheeks getting hot, but she's one of my best friends and I've NEVER called her Loz. Not ever.

'Kieran thought of it,' she says, not looking at me.

My brain whirs as I try to make sense of this.

'Kieran Peters?' I ask her. 'Are you serious?!'

'He's actually really nice, Erin.' Lauren is giving me her stern face now and I want to laugh, except I'm too shocked.

'Er . . . Earth to Lauren. He's a bully and a try-hard and he thinks he's better than everyone else.

And he treats girls like they're a piece of rubbish. Tell me you're not going out with him. Please!'

Lauren's face is flushed a deep red, but she stares at me so hard that for a moment I don't recognize her.

'You don't even know him,' she tells me. Her voice is quiet.

'That's the whole point,' I howl at her. 'I don't want to. And neither did you, before.'

'Before what?' says Lauren. 'Before you got yourself grounded and wasted your entire summer holiday? Before you started moping around the place, going on and on about your awful life? Before the only thing you could talk about was your mum leaving? The rest of us have got a life, Erin. And things change. They just do. Deal with it.'

I stand there, listening to Lauren's words and feeling shock roll over me. She's never spoken to me like that before. I don't know what to say to her so we stand in silence, looking at each other and wondering how it has come to this.

'I'm sorry about what I said about your mum,' says Lauren eventually. 'I know it's been really tough.' I nod, still unable to speak. 'I just couldn't stand you talking about Kieran like that. He's OK, you know – once you understand him.'

There is no part of me that has any desire to understand why Kieran Peters behaves the way that he does. I just know that I've heard the way he talks about people and I was there last year when he punched a kid from Year 7 in the face and broke his glasses. And I've read too many bits of graffiti on the bus stop outside the school gates, where he writes about the girls he's dumped. Kieran Peters loves himself more than he could ever love anybody else in the whole wide world, and I can't bear to watch Lauren build him up only to be flung down when he gets bored of her.

But I can tell that she doesn't want to hear anything I've got to say. And best friends stick together, through thick, thin *and* Kieran Peters. I need to learn to keep my opinion to myself, I guess.

The bedroom door opens and Nat comes racing in. She takes one look at our faces and stops still, her hand flying up to her mouth.

'You told her, then?' she asks Lauren, who nods.

'Oh, I'm so glad you know!' shrieks Nat. 'It's been horrible keeping secrets from you, but Lauren wanted to tell you herself. In person. I think it must be true love!'

Nat giggles and I wonder about the possibility of an alien abduction.

'Anyway, we can't stand around here all day gossiping,' she says, clapping her hands together. 'Loz, Kieran's looking for you.'

Lauren takes a step towards the door but Nat stops her. 'I told him you'd be down in ten minutes. He said to tell you he'd be waiting for you!'

Lauren grins – a daft, goofy grin that normally I would tease her about. Now, though, I stay quiet. Nat picks up a dress from the bed and holds it in front of me.

'Try this on,' she instructs me. I look down at myself and snort.

'Are you joking?' I ask her. 'Please tell me you're joking. I am NOT going out in public wearing THAT!'

Nat looks hurt. 'Why not? What's wrong with it?'

I raise my eyebrows. 'Come on! It's seriously short, it's a colour that I can only describe as *tangerine* and it looks like someone has thrown a tub of glitter on it.'

'I bought this last week with my allowance,' says Nat. 'I was actually being *kind* saying that you could wear it. It's brand new.'

Oh. There's not a lot I can say to this. Fortunately, Lauren takes pity on me.

'Then you should definitely keep it for you to wear next week to Kieran's party,' she tells Nat. 'Anyway, I think Erin would look amazing in that green top you've got.'

'Ooh, yes,' agrees Nat. One of the great things about Nat is that she doesn't get offended very easily. Sometimes I think that's because she doesn't actually realize that she *should* be offended. Whatever the reason, it makes her a good friend.

Nat goes over to her chest of drawers and Lauren looks at me.

'We OK?' she mouths.

I smile at her. 'Yes,' I nod and give her a thumbs up. The three of us have been friends since preschool and we've had plenty of arguments before. This isn't any different to those times. It'll all be forgotten by tomorrow.

Nat comes back over to me and to show willing I pull off my perfectly fine T-shirt and slip on the green top she is handing me. Then I look in the mirror. I look like the backdrop from *A Midsummer Night's Dream*, which was our school production last year. The top is mostly green but there's something shimmery about the material that makes it look like a forest. The sparkly silver gems that are scattered over the front make it look like fairies are having a party on my stomach. I look utterly ridiculous.

'What do you think?' asks Nat anxiously.

'Yeah. No. I'm not loving it,' I tell her, clamping my teeth together to try and stop the scream of horror that I can feel building in my throat. I want this afternoon to go well, I really do, but it all seems to be going a bit wrong and I don't know how to stop it.

'Well, that's because you've got the wrong trousers on,' says Lauren.

Before I can stop them, they have made me change from my old, comfortable, practical-for-a-barbecue jeans into a pair of skin-tight, black leather trousers.

'Yes!' exclaims Nat. 'Doesn't she look perfect, Loz!'

'You look great,' Lauren tells me.

'I don't think this is really *me*,' I tell them, my voice sounding strangled, which is odd as it's my waist that is currently being so constricted by the tight trousers that I can barely breathe.

'That's the whole point,' Lauren says. 'This is the new you!'

'These trousers look like they've been spray-painted on,' I whimper. 'I think they're a bit small for me.'

'They're meant to be like that,' says Nat. 'It's called fashion! Honestly, Erin, do you walk around with your eyes closed?'

Evidently yes, because I have never seen ANYBODY looking the way I look right now.

'Right, come on!' says Nat. 'We don't want to keep Kieran and Dom waiting any longer.'

'Who's Dom?' I ask as we start down the stairs. 'Don't tell me you've got a new boyfriend too!'

Nat laughs. 'Dom's not my boyfriend, silly! I'm with Ashley – you know, Kieran's friend in Year 11. I told you that on the phone weeks ago! The phone call where you hung up on me, actually.'

'Of course you are,' I mutter, but quietly so that they don't hear me. That must have been the day that I was with Martha in the garden. The day that I left her on her own so I could chat to Nat. The memory makes me feel cold and I push it away. 'So who's this Dom, then?'

'Just someone we think you should meet,' says Lauren from behind me.

I stop exactly where I am and turn round to look up at her.

'Oh no,' I tell her, shaking my head. 'I don't think so.'

'Come on, Erin!' says Lauren. 'We've spent ages setting this up. It's your birthday surprise! Dom's lovely – he plays football with Kieran and we thought it'd be really nice if we could all hang out together when term starts again.'

'You're trying to match-make me and you didn't even tell me?' I'm feeling really stupid now and feeling stupid makes me angry. I grip the banister tightly.

'Well, would you have turned up if we'd told you?' asks Lauren. I glare at her and she grins. 'There you go, then.'

I move up a step, ready to push past her and return to the safety of Nat's room and my own clothes, when Lauren deals the killer blow.

'We just wanted to figure out a way to stay the three of us,' she tells me. 'Now I'm with Kieran and Nat's with Ashley. We didn't want you to feel left out. You only have to talk to him. And we've made you a birthday cake and everything.'

I think for a moment. If I leave now I can kiss goodbye to being part of our group. Lauren and Nat are obviously moving on and they're giving me this chance to move on with them. It'd be rude to walk out when they've gone to so much effort. What's the worst thing that can happen?

Lauren can see that I'm not sure and she takes her opportunity.

'We've missed you, Erin,' she says. 'Just come down and talk to Dom. He's really looking forward to meeting you and we'll be right there with you.'

'You promise?' I ask her, turning to look at Nat.

'Absolutely,' says Nat, and Lauren squeezes my shoulder.

I sigh and continue on down the staircase, thankful that at least my feet are larger than Nat's and she had no choice but to let me keep my battered old trainers on. My feet are the only part of me that feel normal right now.

The next two hours pass more slowly than I can believe is possible. I may actually have to pay attention in my next physics lesson to see if there is some kind of phenomenon which means that when you are having the most boring time of your life, the clocks all slow down. I know that sounds super-ungrateful and that I don't deserve to have any friends, but it's just not much fun when all their time is dominated by needy, possessive boyfriends.

The second we emerge through the kitchen door, Kieran pounces on Lauren. It's like he's a cat who's been waiting outside a mouse hole for the poor little mouse to leave its home. Nat dashes off to get more burgers for the barbecue and I am left standing alone and looking everywhere except right next to me where Kieran is slurping at Lauren's face as if she is a Mr Whippy ice cream. It's actually quite disgusting and I admire her self-restraint. If it were me, I would be wiping my mouth with my sleeve.

Things get worse when Nat returns with burgers, Ashley and a boy, who I can only suppose, is Dom. On the positive side, even Kieran cannot eat a burger AND slobber all over Lauren, so there is a brief commercial break from the love-fest that they seem to be starring in. On the negative side, Kieran does seem to feel that he is very capable of eating a burger and talking. And everyone always said that boys can't multitask.

After two minutes, the sight of his half-chewed burger swilling around his mouth while he talks/shouts about fascinating details of his life, such as his new football strip and how his mum thinks he should sign up to be a male model, is starting to make me feel sick, so I turn away.

This is a mistake because I manage to turn right into the path of Dom. Who wants to talk. To me. About me. I get the feeling he has taken a class on how to get a girlfriend, but is possibly only on lesson one. He asks me lots of questions but doesn't want to listen to the answers. He also seems to want to make eye contact with me ALL OF THE TIME. Like, if I look away while I'm thinking of what to say, when I look back he is still staring fixedly at me. It's a bit odd and I'm left undecided about whether it's because he's nervous or a bit odd or is just trying to avoid being blinded by the hideous top I'm wearing.

After a while, Kieran has had enough of talking about himself and decides to return to his other favourite hobby. Luckily, this time he has the decency to drag Lauren off to the bottom of the garden.

'See,' Lauren whispers in my ear as he pulls her past me. 'I told you Kieran was lovely. I KNEW you'd love him when you got to know him!'

I just nod and smile when Nat comes over and whispers to me that she'll just be a few minutes and will I be OK with Dom? Then her and Ashley retreat to a couple of chairs on the patio and start kissing. As Ashley hasn't actually said a single word in the last two hours, I'm sort of relieved to see that his mouth does actually work.

I spend the next ten minutes answering Dom's increasingly bizarre questions about my life.

Then I do a mean thing.

'Could you possibly get me a burger?' I ask Dom.

'No problem,' says Dom, and off he goes.

And off I go, first into the kitchen where I find a scrap of paper and write a quick note to Nat, telling her that I've had to go but thanks for the party. I put it up on the fridge with the monster magnet that I bought Nat last Christmas and then I creep outside and head straight over to the fence where Picasso is lying in the shade. I quickly untie his lead and without looking back we unlatch the gate and escape down the path.

Dad is surprised to see me when he gets home, but I can tell he's pleased.

'I didn't think you'd be back for hours,' he says, flopping down on to the sofa next to me. I'm glad that I managed to arrive home just before him and change out of Nat's awful clothes. Dad would have had a nervous breakdown on the spot if he'd seen me wearing that stuff. 'How was the party?'

'Fine,' I tell him. 'Thanks for the present.'

He glances up at the shelf where the iPad is sitting in its box. 'Did you get it working OK?' he asks.

'Yeah, it's great,' I say. 'What's for tea?'

Dad offers to take me out for a meal but I don't really want to leave the house now I'm home. In the end we settle for pizza delivery and Dad downloads us a film to watch.

'I don't want to be late tomorrow,' I tell him, munching on my stuffed crust and trying not to squirt tomato sauce everywhere.

Dad looks at me. 'About that,' he says. 'I've been thinking. You've done your punishment and you haven't moaned – not too much, anyway! I think you've learnt your lesson. The rest of the summer is yours. You don't have to come back to Oak Hill with me.'

'But I want to.' The words are out of my mouth before I've even had time to think about what I'm saying. 'I can't just abandon Martha, and there's Frog and everything. We've got stuff to do.'

Dad looks surprised but smiles at me and picks up another slice of pizza.

'Well, it's your choice,' he tells me. 'Just come in when you want to.'

*

Later, in bed, I think about today. I've spent the last few weeks thinking that all I wanted was to spend time with Lauren and Nat. But today wasn't that great. They're still my friends and all that, but I didn't feel like I feel when I'm at Oak Hill. Like anything might happen.

Mostly, the problem with today was that I missed Martha. And I missed Frog. And I wished that I was spending my birthday with them.

DIMPLED CHEEKS*

'Are you one hundred per cent sure about this?' I ask Frog doubtfully.

'Totally,' he tells me. 'How hard can it be?'

I'm not sure what to say to this. There are many answers desperate to fly out of my mouth, including 'ludicrously hard', 'insanely difficult' and 'harder than a hard rock', but I don't think he'd appreciate my lack of team spirit, and he's obviously gone to some effort.

* *Dimpled Cheeks* (1955) by Jean Dubuffet. This artist used butterfly wings as a collage to make a picture of an old lady. The wings totally look like that weird browny-orange material that old ladies like to wear. She looks kind, though, even though she is made out of dead animals. She makes me think that she'd be a good listener if you needed a friendly ear.

Frog puts his hands on his hips, legs apart and raises his eyebrows at me.

'Is that your *I'm-about-to-dance* pose?' I tease him. 'Very convincing!'

'Are you going to sit there all day or are we going to give this a go?' he asks me.

'Sit here all day?' I try, but the scowl on his face makes it clear that this was the wrong answer. 'Erm – give it a go?' I say and Frog grins.

I sigh, but get up off the bench and walk over to the patch of grass where he's waiting.

'What do we do first?'

Frog pauses, his forehead wrinkled up as he tries to remember. 'I think we have to face each other and hold hands.'

I surreptitiously wipe my palms on my jeans, just in case they're sweaty. I'm suddenly feeling a bit nervous, even though it's just Frog and we're the only ones here.

'Like this?' I ask, and stretch my hands out towards him. 'Now what?'

'Well, we have to move our feet really fast and take lots of tiny steps.'

We start bouncing up and down on the spot. 'And then I swing you out to the side, like this.'

Frog lets go of one of my hands and pulls me hard with the other hand and I swing out next to him. Not bad for a beginner!

'And then you go under my arm and I spin you round and –'

I trip over his foot and go down on to the ground like a sack of potatoes.

'Ow!' I shout. 'Why did you do that?'

'Are you OK?' asks Frog, crouching next to me. I'm actually fine but then I take a look at his face with his scruffy hair flopped over one eye. I can see he's trying not to laugh, which makes me cross.

'No,' I tell him grumpily. 'I think I've broken something.'

'Like what? The world record for the shortest jitterbug ever!'

'It was a stupid idea to begin with,' I tell him, rubbing my elbow. 'There's no way we can learn to jitterbug. And if Martha had seen that little performance she might have actually died laughing. I bet she wouldn't even recognize it as the jitterbug.'

'We can't just give up,' says Frog. 'We've only just started.'

When I met up with Frog this morning he was buzzing with excitement for his new plan. He dragged me to the computer room at Oak Hill (a tiny cupboard with one computer inside that nobody ever uses) and made me watch a YouTube clip of people doing the jitterbug dance. He said that it'd be really great if we learnt to jitterbug so that we could show Martha and remind her of the good old days. I wasn't convinced but, as I'm starting to discover, Frog is the kind of person it's hard to say 'no' to.

Frog stands up and reaches down to me. Reluctantly I take his hand and let him pull me to my feet. I am officially the world's worst dancer and I have a nasty feeling that no good is going to come of this.

'Again,' he says and assumes his start position. I take hold of both his hands and this time, I manage to bounce on the spot, swing to the side, go under his arm AND kick my leg out to the left before I collapse in a heap.

'What happened then?' moans Frog. 'We were getting somewhere that time.'

'I tripped!' I snap.

'What on? A blade of grass? Come ON, make a bit of effort, Erin.'

I stand up and glare at him. 'It'd help if we had some music,' I say. 'And if you could keep your canoe-size feet under control.'

'Again,' dictates Frog. 'And one, two, three, four!'

We begin our routine but this time we're stopped before I can gain yet another bruise on my backside. The sound of clapping comes from the path and when I look across I see Beatrice clapping while, in front of her, Martha bangs one hand against her leg, a huge grin on her face.

'Looking good, kids!' calls Beatrice, wheeling Martha over to the bench. I scowl at her and let go of Frog's hand. We walk to the bench and sit down next to Martha.

'I'll be back later,' says Beatrice.

'We'll bring Martha up to the house in a while,' Frog tells her. 'If that's OK?'

Beatrice glances at Martha and then nods. 'Don't stay out too late!' she tells her, and then she sticks her hands in her pockets and strolls back down the path, whistling as she goes.

Martha jerks her head at us and then across at the grass. It's obvious she wants us to tell her what we were doing.

'Don't ask,' I say. 'We're terrible at dancing.'

'We were trying to learn the jitterbug, so that we could surprise you,' says Frog. 'But it's impossible. I have no idea how you used to do it when you were young.'

Martha grins and I notice that her smile isn't as lopsided as it usually is. Maybe she's actually been doing her exercises. That or I'm just getting used to the way she looks.

'We've found some clips on YouTube, though, of people dancing the jitterbug. Shall we go inside and you can watch them?'

Martha shakes her head. That would be a definite 'no' then. I sink on to the bench. We're going to have to come up with some better ideas if we want to cheer her up and motivate her to get better.

'Really?' Frog is saying. I glance at him and see he is looking at Martha. 'I'm not sure that's a good idea.'

Martha is sitting up straight in her chair and is using her left hand to point first at Frog and then at me. And then at the patch of grass where we were dancing.

'Oh no,' I tell her. 'You saw us. It's not going to work, Martha.'

Martha scowls at me and points again.

'I think she really wants us to try,' Frog whispers to me.

'I don't care WHAT she wants,' I say loudly. 'I am not humiliating myself again, just so that she can have a good laugh.'

Martha sniggers silently. I've had quite enough of being laughed at for one day. I turn on her.

'I CANNOT DANCE!' I say very slowly and loudly, as if I'm talking to someone who doesn't understand English. 'I don't DO dancing. I tried. I failed. End of conversation.'

Martha drops her head and looks up at us through her eyelashes. Her eyes look all pleading and she reminds me of Picasso when he wants me to throw him a ball.

'Come on, Erin,' says Frog. 'It'll make her happy.'

'She's manipulating us,' I tell him, and turn to her. 'I know exactly what you're doing and it won't work. You might as well get up and dance with Frog yourself.'

'Erin!' Frog sounds shocked but I ignore him. I'm too busy looking at the steely glint in Martha's eyes and as I watch she yanks at the blanket that is tucked over her legs and throws it on the ground, scattering her notepad on to the ground.

Frog spins round at the sound and together we stare as Martha swings first one leg and then the other off the footrest of her wheelchair. Then, using her left hand, she braces against the side of the chair and pushes herself up to a standing position.

Frog and I both surge forward at the same time but she jerks her head at us and it's easy to tell that she wants us to stop.

We hover, either side of her, close but not touching, as she lets go of the chair and pulls herself upright. She takes one step forward and wobbles. I hear myself gasp and I desperately want to hold on to her arm, but I don't. Instead, I watch as she takes a second step and then another. Then her left arm rises and she turns her head to look at Frog.

Frog is frozen in position. Martha smiles at him and he doesn't move until I hiss 'Frog!' at him. Then he springs into action, moving in front of Martha and reaching out to take her hand. I can tell that he's taking quite a lot of her weight because both of their knuckles are clenched and white, but neither of them speak as Martha moves slowly forward and then under Frog's arm. Every single step she takes is laborious and considered – it looks as if she's having to force her brain to send the right messages to her feet, but at the same time she somehow manages to look graceful. She moves out to the side and Frog copies her and in that instant, their arms outstretched and heads turned looking towards each other, I can see Martha the dancer. I can imagine her doing these moves, but sped up about twenty times, and I can see the energy and enthusiasm and passion that she would have had.

And then her right leg starts to shake and I grab the wheelchair and quickly push it up behind her and Frog helps lower her down until she's safely sitting on the chair. I breathe out loudly and realize that I'd been holding my breath since she stood up.

'Are you OK?' Frog asks her, worry seeping out through his voice.

'I'm SO sorry,' I tell her, coming round in front of her wheelchair and looking down. 'I didn't mean to sound unkind.'

'Are you OK?' repeats Frog, and Martha nods. Then she looks over and points at me.

'I know,' I tell her. 'I AM sorry.' I can feel tears prickling at the backs of my eyes and then, before I can do anything to stop them, they start overflowing and trickling down my cheeks.

I turn away quickly, desperate to hide, but it's too late. I feel Frog's hand on my shoulder but I can't turn to face them. I can't believe that I taunted Martha and nearly made her fall over AGAIN. It's like the only thing I can ever do is get everything wrong.

'It's OK, Erin,' Frog whispers gently. 'Come on, just look at her.'

I shake my head and rub furiously at my eyes. Frog puts both hands on my shoulders and twists me round and when I look at Martha I can see a big grin covering her face.

'I'm sorry,' I repeat and she shakes her head, as if these aren't the words she was looking for.

'Come on, Erin. No cry face,' says Frog. 'Martha isn't telling you off. She's asking you to do something.'

I watch as Martha, her eyes never leaving mine, jabs her finger at me again and then at Frog and then back at the grass.

'Yes!' I say, feeling my body sag in relief. 'I'll dance if you really want me to.'

Frog wheels Martha's chair under the shade of a tree and I take a moment to compose myself, my mind working overtime to figure out what just happened. I'm not proud of myself for provoking her but look what Martha just did! She stood up and walked and everything! I think that, massively by mistake, we might have just discovered the way to get Martha working on her recovery. Maybe she needs a bit of that *tough love* that people go on about.

'She can't resist a challenge!' I whisper to Frog as we walk across to the grassy area. 'We can totally use that to get her talking and using the right side of her body.'

We stand facing each other and Frog reaches out to take my hands. Martha bangs the side of her chair and moves her right hand to the side.

'Are you saying that we need to stand further apart?' I call. She nods and we both take a few steps back. 'This would be a lot easier if you could just tell us,' I shout to her.

'Seriously, Erin, you're playing with fire,' hisses Frog. 'My nerves can't stand another "Martha Challenge" right now.'

I grin at him and turn back to where Martha is sitting.

'Just don't expect anything great. Or coordinated. Or that looks like actual dancing,' I tell her. 'Because I am NOT a good dancer.'

CRACKED EARTH
REMOVED*

It's been Eighty-one Days Without Mum and I'm really missing her. I want to tell her about Dom and the party and ask what I should do about Lauren and Nat. I didn't realize how hurt they'd be when I ran off without saying a proper goodbye. They'd made me a cake and everything and I kind of messed up all their plans. I guess I thought they

* *Cracked Earth Removed* (1986) by Andy Goldsworthy. I suppose that this is kind of a sculpture. The artist found some ground where the earth was all cracked and took away certain pieces. Probably everybody thought he was mad but he knew what he wanted. He kept going and then, when you see it from above, it looks like an entire world. He took something away and made a totally new thing. This makes me think that sometimes, it's worth trying something new. Just to see what happens.

wouldn't notice – that they had plenty of new friends and wouldn't miss me. They've been texting me loads and asking what happened. I've tried to explain but I'm not sure what I can say that will make them understand how I feel. I'm not even certain how I DO feel. I just know that them trying to set me up with Dom made me uncomfortable – even more uncomfortable than the leather trousers that they made me wear.

Dad let me go over to Nat's the day after to return the trousers and get my own clothes back. I said I was sorry but Nat was quite sniffy with me and I suppose I can't really blame her. I got it wrong. Again. And now I'm going to have exactly no friends when school starts back in September.

I'm trying not to think miserable thoughts today, though, because I'm meant to be meeting Frog to hear his next big idea for our Martha Challenge. I really, really hope that this one doesn't involve me making a complete idiot of myself, like the dancing. Martha's been forcing us to practise the jitterbug every day and I don't think we're getting any better. It's really difficult dancing without music.

Frog has asked me to meet him in the day room, which is where his grandad spends most of his time. I've said hello to him a couple of times now and he seems quite nice, but I'm not really sure how much he can understand and I don't want to confuse him. Hoping that Frog has already arrived I push open the door and then stand still in surprise.

The day room is heaving with people. Old people. And it's VERY loud. Looking around I can't see Frog anywhere and for a second I nearly turn and leave, certain that I've just gatecrashed a pensioners' get-together. Then I hear someone call my name and when I stand on tiptoe I can see Frog on the other side of the room, beckoning to me and laughing.

I hesitate a moment longer. There are a LOT of people in here and I'm really only interested in Martha. But I want to see Frog so I slip through the crowd, dodging walking frames and sticks and sliding between armchairs until I'm standing next to him.

'What's going on?' I ask him, peering around. Everyone seems to be looking in the same direction and I can't work out what's so interesting because all I can see in front of me is a lot of grey hair and bald heads.

'Isn't it brilliant!' yells Frog. He needs to yell because, for a bunch of old people, they certainly know how to make some noise.

'What?' I shriek back. 'Isn't *what* brilliant?'

'That,' shouts Frog and he points to the front of the room. I turn to look and at that moment the crowd parts slightly and I see Martha, sitting in her wheelchair and playing tennis. Against Frog's grandad. And from the looks of things she is completely annihilating him.

I look back at Frog, my mouth gaping open. 'What . . .? How . . .?'

'I brought it in from home,' Frog tells me proudly. 'I thought of it after the other day when you said that Martha can't resist a challenge. Look at her backhand!'

I push my way through the Oak Hill residents who are yelling encouragement at the players and stand by Martha's chair. She glances up at me briefly but then looks straight back at the TV screen, her focus utterly on the tennis game.

'Looks like you're doing OK,' I tell her.

She nods and grins and then leans across to rally a particularly demon serve that Frog's grandad has just dished up.

'Hey, watch out!' I yelp, leaping to the side just before she sideswipes me with the Wii controller.

On the screen, the tennis ball whizzes through the air and even though Frog's grandad tries his best to reach it, he misses and the point goes to Martha. The crowd goes wild.

'Game, set and match!' shouts one old man, leaping out of his chair in excitement. I look at him in alarm – I'm not sure he should be doing that at his age.

Martha passes the Wii controller to the lady next to her and then wheels herself slowly over to Frog's grandad. She stretches out her left arm and they shake hands, grinning at each other.

'It's been a while since I've played tennis,' he tells her. 'I enjoyed that. Maybe we'll have a rematch one of these days?'

Martha smiles and nods at him and then I push her wheelchair carefully through the mass of people who are demanding that Frog sets up the Wii so that they can go bowling. We find a space at the back of the room and I sit down next to Martha, watching as Frog explains the rules.

'You're pretty good at tennis,' I say to Martha. 'Did you play when you were younger?'

She nods at me and then smiles at Frog as he emerges from the crowd and flops down on to the chair next to me. He's laughing.

'I didn't think I was going to make it out alive,' he says. 'It's a good job you can attach the controllers to their wrists – Doris can't remember to hold on to it and every time she bowls she throws it at the TV!'

'This was a really good idea,' I tell him. 'They all love it!'

'Well, it was just sitting around at home. Nobody really goes on it any more and Mum said that it was OK to bring it here for the rest of the summer. Just on a loan.'

I turn to look at Martha. She looks a bit warm – her face is flushed and her breathing is quite fast and her eyes are shining like she's excited. She points towards the TV and starts to push herself forward, but I'm worried that it's all been a bit much for her.

'Maybe you should have a rest for a while?' I ask her. My answer is an instant scowl.

'Do you want to go back on the Wii?' Frog asks. 'We could play baseball next!' His reward is a beaming smile.

I'm not convinced that she hasn't overdone it, though, and the last thing I want is for Martha to get ill, so I get up and fetch a glass of water from the table by the door.

'You need to drink this,' I tell her.

She reaches out her left hand and very, very slowly brings the glass to her lips. I want to help her but I can tell that she won't appreciate me interfering so I try to look as if I'm not paying her any attention. I can see, though, out of the corner of my eye, that the water is almost all going into her mouth, with only a tiny bit dribbling on to her chin.

I turn to her as she starts to lower her arm and as I take the glass from her our hands touch. Martha's skin is warm and soft and I feel a jolt of something rush through me. It takes me by surprise and I busy myself taking the glass back to the table for a bit longer than necessary as I try to figure out what it is.

When I look back to where we were sitting, and see Frog casually dabbing at Martha's chin with a tissue like it's no big deal, I realize what it is that I'm feeling. It feels warm. It feels safe. It feels right. It feels like I might, just a little bit, love these two people.

HERE I AM, HERE I STAY*

Martha has disappeared. Frog and I wait for her for ages in the garden but she just doesn't turn up.

'Where do you think she is?' I ask Frog.

He shakes his head. 'I don't know. You don't think she's left, do you?'

'What d'you mean *left*?' I say. 'Where could she have gone?'

* *Here I Am, Here I Stay* (1990) by Louise Bourgeois. A pair of feet in a glass box, on top of a big slab of marble. Some people might think that this is a bit weird and if I'm honest, so do I – but in a good way. It makes me think about how amazing humans can be. How, if we're determined enough, we can do almost anything. Some people don't have staying power and they think it's OK to leave. This sculpture reminds me that not everybody goes. Some people stay with you, no matter what.

'Maybe she's living in a different care home?' suggests Frog, but he doesn't sound very convinced.

'This is stupid.' I get to my feet and pull Frog with me. 'We need to track down Beatrice and find out where she is.'

We walk down the path, intent on heading up to the house where Beatrice is bound to be sitting with one of the old people. We don't get there, though, because just as we're about to turn the corner I hear voices ahead of us.

'Well, you say that like it's easy, but Martha is one of the most stubborn women I've ever met.'

I freeze and Frog walks straight into the back of me. He lets out an *oomph* sound and I turn quickly, shushing him with my finger on his lips. His eyes open wide in surprise but he stands still and I turn back towards the hedge and creep a bit closer, Frog right behind me.

An unfamiliar voice laughs loudly and then I hear someone we know.

'It must be so hard for her, though. I gather she was a very independent lady before the stroke.' I can hear the concern in Beatrice's voice even from here. She properly cares about Martha and not just because it's her job.

'Well, what about her family?' asks the other person. Her voice has a hardness that is putting me on edge. I hope she doesn't have anything to do with looking after Martha. She doesn't sound kind. 'It's all very well shelling out to send them here but a visit every now and again wouldn't go amiss. Take the pressure off us a bit too. We're not paid enough to be their friends.'

'She hasn't got any family,' says Beatrice. 'And actually, I don't need paying to be Martha's friend. She's a fascinating, funny lady when you stop and get to know her.'

If I pull apart the leaves in front of me and squint with one eye I can just make out two pairs of feet, a few metres away. Beatrice is obviously on a break with one of the other care workers. As I watch, something is thrown to the ground and a foot stamps on it and grinds it into the path. The smell of cigarette wafts over the hedge and it reminds me of the first and last time I tried to smoke. The first time that I met Martha. Even the memory makes me want to cough.

'Oh, don't give me that.' Uncaring sounds annoyed. 'Everyone's got family somewhere – especially if they can afford to live somewhere like Oak Hill. There's got to be some distant relative sniffing about for a slice of her cash when she's gone.'

I feel Frog stiffen next to me and then he too makes a gap in the hedge so that he can do his own spying.

'Well, she hasn't,' says Beatrice in a firm-sounding voice. I don't think she likes Uncaring very much. 'She lost her childhood sweetheart, Tommy, in the war. They didn't have time to start their lives together before it was all over. No chance of children and she never fell in love again. When she first arrived here she wrote down that she had a younger sister, but she died ten years ago. She has nobody left.'

'I suppose that accounts for her being the way she is, then.' Uncaring sounds as if she knows she's narked Beatrice off and she's trying to be nice, but it clearly doesn't come naturally to her. 'And she may well be *fascinating*, but she's also the most devious, cunning old woman I've ever met. Lording it up in that wheelchair! She could walk if she put her mind to it – she just wants to make us push her around all day. If she'd only put more effort into her exercises then she could be talking and walking like everyone else. Mrs Thompson is just waiting for her to mess up again so that we can send her packing. She's not exactly the type of resident we want at Oak Hill, is she? Far too high-maintenance.'

'She's very unwell and there's nothing to motivate her,' says Beatrice sadly. 'I just think she can't see the point in fighting any more. Since her stroke it's all been too hard, and this new illness is just too much. She doesn't want to leave her room or see anyone. I'm really worried that she isn't going to rally from this. This could be the end for her.'

There's a sudden movement and Beatrice's legs come into view as she stands up. We both let go of the leaves and the hedge snaps back into place as we hear both women walk away down the path, conversation about the weather drifting back to us on the breeze.

I turn to look at Frog. 'Did you hear all that?'

He nods. 'That care worker talking to Beatrice is *mean*! She didn't sound as if she even likes old people.'

'Never mind that.' I march down the path, Frog running after me to keep up. 'Didn't you hear what they said about Martha? She's really ill. We have to do something to help.'

'Like what?' Frog asks, puffing away behind me as I speed-walk towards Dad's shed.

I don't answer him until we've reached the shed and sat down, our backs against the side.

'Like what, Erin?' repeats Frog. 'What's the plan?'

'I don't know yet,' I reluctantly admit. 'But neither of us is leaving here until we've figured something out. We can't just abandon Martha and you heard what Beatrice said. She needs something to motivate her, something that will make her do her exercises and help her get better. She needs cheering up or she might not be OK. She might even die. Now – no speaking until one of us has got an idea.'

We sit, just thinking, for what feels like ages. After about four minutes, Frog cracks.

'We could bake her a cake?' he suggests.

I tut. 'Duh! How is *that* going to cheer her up? It's not very special, is it?'

'Well, you think of something better then, mastermind.' He scowls at me and folds his arms. 'Come on.'

'I am *thinking*,' I tell him. 'Shush.'

My brain is whizzing through hundreds of ideas. I think about what Mum used to do for me if I was unwell, but I don't think having a blanket nest on the sofa and watching *Bedknobs and Broomsticks* will have the same appeal to Martha. I actually used to quite like being unwell because it was the only time Mum would let Picasso into the living room. Snuggling up with him and feeling his warm little body cuddled up next to me under the blanket was the best feeling in the world. Even when I'm well, stroking him and sensing how much more he loves me with each stroke makes me feel happier than I can describe.

'How about if –' starts Frog but I hold my hand up to stop him. I know I seem rude but there's a thought flitting round the edges of my brain and I need him to be quiet if I'm going to catch it.

'Hang on, hang on,' I say, waving my hands around wildly as if I can literally pluck the idea out of the air. And then I do.

'Picasso!' I breathe, letting the thought fill my head.

'Sorry?' says Frog, utterly confused.

'Stroke! Two different types of stroke! That's what made me think of it. Martha's stroke and stroking a dog. That's called a homophone by the way – I learnt it in school!' I am ranting but I don't care. This is brilliant!

'What are you going on about?' asks Frog, staring at me as if I have lost the plot.

So I take a deep breath and tell him my plan. And Frog agrees that, quite possibly, this is the best idea ever known to mankind and that I, Erin Edwards, may well be the cleverest individual on the planet right now.

THE DOG*

Carrying out my ingenious plan takes some forward thinking and a lot of nerve. My alarm clock goes off earlier than it's ever gone off before and I'm out of bed faster than you can say *#groundedforeverifIgetcaught*.

The keys to Dad's van are on the table in the hall and I've managed to sneak the dog bed out of the kitchen and outside to the van before Dad even comes downstairs. I thought he might be surprised that I was already up but he's got a big

---

* *The Dog* (1957) by Pablo Picasso. My favourite picture EVER. Picasso drew a picture of his dog with just one line but he still managed to exactly sum up how brilliant and fun and loyal his dachshund was. Just like my Picasso. He drew other animals like this too, but I think the dog is his best one (although the camel is actually pretty genius too).

delivery of garden stuff today so he's just pleased that I'm virtually ready to go.

We eat our breakfast in silence, him going through his delivery inventory and me hoping that everything is going to work. I've put the dog bed into a corner of the van and wedged it in place with Dad's toolkit. The last thing I want to happen is for Picasso to be skidding and sliding across the van floor every time we go round a corner.

Today I am a dog smuggler. OK, it might not be on the same level as drug smuggling, but actually, when you think about it, there's loads of drugs at Oak Hill already, what with all the medication the old people are taking. There are no dogs at Oak Hill, though. And I suspect the punishment for taking a dog into a strict *No Animals* environment is probably worse than the punishment for taking drugs in. People can be weird like that. I remember Dad telling me at the start of the summer that he'd lose his job if he allowed me to take Picasso into the grounds. I cross my fingers under the table and hope that I'm not about to make another monumental, Erin-sized mistake.

I offer to wash up while Dad goes to clean his teeth and as soon as he's gone I whistle to Picasso.

He looks up from his breakfast and gives me his daft, doggy smile and then he gets up and pads across the floor on his little legs. I bend down and pick him up and then as quickly and quietly as I possibly can I open the back door and race round the outside of the house to where Dad's van is standing in the drive.

I unlock the double doors and crawl inside. Picasso jumps out of my arms and does that random, running round in a circle thing that I normally find cute and hilarious. Today, though, I don't want to encourage any silly behaviour.

'In your bed,' I whisper, pointing him in the direction of the dog bed. But Picasso isn't having any of it. He skips over to Dad's strimmer and starts sniffing it, his tiny tail wagging as if it's Christmas Day.

'Picasso!' I hiss. 'That is *not* for you! In your bed!'

This time he has the decency to look at me before bounding across to a spade and testing it out with one paw. I've had enough. It's time to get serious before Dad comes out here and my plan is doomed before it's begun.

I crawl further into the van and pick up my excited, crazy dog.

'Do you want a treat?' I ask him. He stops wriggling and I deposit him into the dog bed. 'Then you have to promise to stay there until I come to get you. Understood?'

Picasso gazes at me with his mismatched eyes, his nose pushing into my hands to find the promised treat.

'OK, then. I'll be back really soon. Don't be scared. We're doing the right thing.'

I leave him happily munching on a biscuit and scoot in through the back door just before Dad comes into the kitchen.

'Have you seen my van keys?' he asks, patting his trouser pockets.

I wave them at him. 'I've got them already. We need to get going if you don't want to be late.'

'Thanks, love,' says Dad, and the smile he gives me is so trusting that I feel a moment of guilt. But then I tell myself that I haven't actually lied to him and I haven't taken anything that isn't mine. And that sneaking Picasso into Oak Hill is really the right thing to do to help Martha get better.

The drive to work is agonizing. Every time we go round a corner I cross my fingers tightly and hope like mad that Picasso is OK. As we get closer to Oak Hill my heart starts to race. This part of the plan is less clear to me. It goes something along the lines of *look for a way to distract Dad before he opens up the van*. I am suddenly aware that I perhaps needed to put a bit more thought into this stage, but it's too late now.

We pull in through the gates and up the drive. And salvation is staring me right in the face. Or rather, Frog is. He is waiting for us by the front door and as soon as he sees us he races over to where Dad is parking. Dad barely has a chance to open his door before Frog starts talking, his words coming out in a garbled rush.

'Mr Edwards! I'm so glad you're here! There's a flood in the kitchen and Beatrice doesn't know what to do!'

Dad jumps out of the van and strides towards the back.

'I'd better grab my tools then,' he says.

I stare in desperation at Frog while I struggle to undo my seat belt. Frog is all over the situation, though. He darts past Dad and stands blocking the van doors. I hear him start to speak and I wrench at the seat belt, finally managing to get free. I dive out of the cab and rush round the van.

'. . . to just go straight there,' Frog is saying. 'She said she wants your opinion as soon as possible.'

Poor Dad doesn't stand a chance. He nods at Frog and thanks him and then heads towards the house, ruffling my hair as he walks past.

The second he's out of sight I open up the van doors and get hit in the chest by a furry sausage. I grab it with both hands and the three of us run across the car park and into the trees where we can't be seen.

'What *is* that?' asks Frog, when we stop running.

'It's not a *that*, it's a he,' I say, pretending to be offended. 'This is Picasso. He's a dachshund.'

'He's a sausage dog,' states Frog and we both start laughing because Picasso totally looks like a sausage. He looks like a cartoon dog.

'Dachshund means "badger dog" in German,' I tell Frog.

'That's a way better name than "dachshund", he says. 'Badger dog sounds quite menacing and freaky. You should call him that.'

Picasso gives a little bark and I put him down on the ground.

'Let him sniff you,' I say to Frog, who stands very still while Picasso walks round his feet.

'Why is he doing that?' whispers Frog and I stifle a grin.

'Cos he's trying to figure out what the terrible stink is!' I tell him. Frog glares at me and I see that he actually looks quite worried. 'Haven't you got a dog?' I ask him.

Frog shakes his head. 'My mum says we're not around enough to look after one. I don't know if I really like dogs, to be honest. They always seem a bit . . . I don't know. A bit unpredictable?'

I laugh. 'They are! That's what makes them fun. Look, sit down next to me and meet Picasso properly. He won't hurt you.'

Frog still looks unsure but he walks over to me and we sit down together on the mossy ground. Picasso has a last sniff of Frog and then curls up between us.

'He wants to be stroked,' I tell Frog. 'Look – like this.' I stroke the dog's back with firm, flowing movements and after a moment Frog joins in.

'He's trembling,' he says. 'Is he scared or something?'

'No,' I tell him. 'He thinks he's a cat. He's sighing. He does that if he's happy – a bit like purring!'

Frog smiles and we sit, stroking Picasso and discussing the best way to sneak into the house without being caught.

We've made our plans and I'm just starting to think it's time to act when disaster strikes. One second Picasso is so blissed out he's virtually asleep and the next second he's gone.

'What?' exclaims Frog, leaping to his feet as Picasso shoots away from us, so fast that he's almost a blur.

'Picasso!' I yell, before I remember that he shouldn't be here and that his presence at Oak Hill is classified, need-to-know information. And that absolutely nobody except Frog and me needs to know.

'Where's he gone?' asks Frog, his head spinning round in a useless attempt to spot Picasso.

'Squirrel!' I hiss, taking off at a run. Well, I would be running if it wasn't for all the branches and twigs and lumpy bits of ground that keep trying to trip me up.

Frog overtakes me and I follow him through the trees. We are both trying to move quickly without a) being seen or b) making any noise. This means that we are doing a comedy run, bent double and only landing on our tiptoes. We must look ridiculous.

'When you say *squirrel*,' Frog mutters over his shoulder, 'do you mean an actual squirrel? Like, is that something dogs genuinely get excited about? Cos I thought that was just a joke.'

'I meant an actual squirrel,' I confirm, squinting ahead to see if I can spot Picasso.

'But why would your dog think he had a chance of catching a squirrel?' asks Frog. He's not letting up on this subject and if we don't find Picasso soon then we're in serious trouble. 'I mean, not to be rude or anything, but your dog has a bit of a weight issue going on. I'm fairly sure he couldn't climb a tree. And squirrels are pretty agile.'

There! Up ahead I can see Picasso. I gesture to Frog to circle behind him and I approach nice and slow, using my best calm, reassuring voice.

'Who's a silly dog, then? Who's a very naughty dog that's going to get his owner grounded for the rest of her life if he doesn't start behaving sensibly?'

Picasso looks over at me. He is standing up with his front paws resting against the trunk of a tree. And he is yapping very loudly.

Frog appears from behind the tree and I grab Picasso's collar and pick him up. The yapping gets louder and I look up to see what is causing all the trouble. Frog follows my gaze. There, on a branch above our heads, is a squirrel. It isn't trying to hide and as I watch, it seems to jiggle about from foot to foot.

'Er, Erin?' says Frog.

'Yes, Frog,' I answer.

'You see that squirrel?'

'I do, Frog.'

'I think it's taunting us.'

I look at Frog and then back again at the squirrel. Picasso is going crazy in my arms, as if I am the only thing between him and a squirrel lunch. I am about to tell the stupid squirrel exactly what I think of it when I hear voices and realize that we're closer to the path than I had thought. I have to be content with flinging a rude word in the squirrel's general direction before we dive back into the trees. It is time to regroup and carry out Mission Picasso.

We make it through the grounds without being spotted. I'm wearing a big, baggy hoody and I've managed to zip Picasso inside. If you saw me from a distance you wouldn't even know he was there.

When we get to the side door, Frog goes ahead and uses our pre-agreed sign to let me know it's safe to proceed. We spent ages trying out different signals: rubbing his nose meant 'all clear', coughing meant 'someone's coming', double blink meant 'retreat to safety', alternate winks meant 'stand still'. In the end we decided they were all too confusing so now we're using the sophisticated 'thumbs up' and 'thumbs down' approach, which seems to be working well.

And now we're at Martha's door. Frog has already scoped out Beatrice's position and she's busy in the day room handing out cups of tea. She should be there for ages yet. I knock quietly on the door but there's no sound from within so tentatively, and feeling quite nervous, I nod at Frog and he opens the door just wide enough for us both to slip inside.

The room is in darkness and doesn't smell too fresh. I tiptoe over to the bed where Martha is propped up and bend down over her. Her eyes are open and my first thought is that she must be dead. I gasp and she blinks, and I realize that even though she's obviously alive, she isn't OK.

'Martha,' I whisper. 'It's us. We've come to visit you.'

She doesn't say anything but that's all right. Nothing different to normal. It's her eyes that are bothering me. There's nothing in them. None of the moodiness I saw when I upset her. None of the naughtiness that was there when Beatrice told her off. None of the happiness and excitement she had when she was playing on the Wii. Nothing.

'You try,' I tell Frog and while he attempts to get a response I open the curtains and let the sunlight in. While I'm there I fling open the windows too. I'm not sure if this is what Martha wants but I'm willing to do anything to get a reaction out of her, even if it's a cross one. This zombie Martha is starting to freak me out.

'Any luck?' I ask him when I go back to the bed, but Frog just shakes his head.

'Then it's time,' I say, unzipping my hoody. Frog looks nervous but I know this is the right thing to do. Martha needs something to make her smile. She needs something to cuddle. Picasso is our only hope.

'You know what to do,' I whisper into his floppy, gorgeous ears and then I place him on the bottom of her bed. Frog and I back away until we're standing right next to the door and watch.

Picasso turns round a few times to get his bearings and then he spots Martha. She hasn't seen him yet but as he gently navigates his way across the blanket she obviously feels him because her head turns slightly and her eyes open a little wider in surprise.

Picasso trots right over to the head of the bed, where he stops. Resting his front paws on the propped-up pillow he raises himself until he is level with Martha's head. The two of them look at each other for a long time. I can feel Frog next to me, holding his breath, and I do the same, desperate for this to work. Desperate for Martha to see that there are good things here. Things worth getting better for.

After a while, Picasso lowers his paws. My heart starts to sink until I see that he has no plans to leave Martha. He turns round very carefully so as not to stand on her, and then tenderly snuggles down into the crook of her right arm. Martha looks across at me for the first time and I take a step forward.

'His name's Picasso,' I tell her. 'He loves being stroked more than anything in the world.'

Martha looks from me to Frog and I see something flare up in her eyes just for a second. Then she looks down at Picasso and slowly, haltingly, she brings her left hand up and across in order to stroke Picasso's back. He shudders slightly in his happy-dog way and settles further into the bed. And I lean against Frog and watch as Martha starts to come back from whatever lonely, miserable place she's been in for the last few days.

It's my fault. I forget to keep an eye on the time. Frog and I end up sitting on Martha's bed and chatting quietly while she strokes Picasso and he shamelessly cuddles up to her, enjoying all the attention. I'm explaining to Frog that Picasso is not your usual dachshund.

'Dachshunds aren't supposed to like strangers,' I tell him. 'But I don't think Picasso got that particular memo because he likes everyone. Especially if they play with him or feed him.'

'I wouldn't mind having –' begins Frog but he is rudely interrupted by the door flying open and a very irate Beatrice stomping in.

'Who gave you two permission to come in here?' she asks, her voice cross. 'Martha doesn't want any visitors at the moment. You can't just waltz in here whenever you feel like it.'

She approaches the bed, glaring at us. I scoot closer to Frog, hoping to block Picasso from her sight.

'I'm sorry, Martha,' she says. 'They had no right to just –'

She's seen him. Her forehead wrinkles in a frown and her eyes narrow. I smile at her, hoping to win her over. After all, we're only in here because we care about Martha, just like she does.

It doesn't work.

'What is *that*?' she asks, although it's one of those rhetorical questions that aren't really a question. Beatrice already knows the answer. She's not stupid – and even if Picasso is more sausage than dog it's fairly obvious that he is an animal. And therefore banned from Oak Hill.

'This is –' I start but Beatrice slams her hand up in front of me, barely missing my nose, and I stop speaking.

'You have got to be kidding me,' she mutters under her breath. 'You kids brought a *dog* in *here*?'

She turns her steely glare first on me and then on Frog.

'Up!' she barks and we both leap off the bed.

'We thought –' says Frog but I elbow him in the ribs and he shuts up. I can tell that this is no time for trying to justify our actions.

'Unbelievable,' murmurs Beatrice. I'm not sure if she's talking to us or to herself so I don't say anything, but the three of us stand in a line and stare at the bed. Martha hasn't stopped stroking Picasso but she is looking at Beatrice. And her eyes look like they're throwing Beatrice a challenge.

Beatrice sighs and lets her shoulders slump forward. She looks tired for a moment but then she straightens herself and turns to look at us.

'This calls for some damage limitation,' she says. 'Get that dog out of here before anyone sees you.'

She's not going to tell on us. All we have to do is sneak back to the van with Picasso and we'll be home and dry! I risk a quick grin at Frog and take a step towards the bed.

'What on earth is going on in here?' shrieks a voice from the doorway. A voice that I know I've heard before. It's hard and cold and bossy, just like it was yesterday in the garden when she was talking to Beatrice.

I spin round to see Uncaring striding into the room. She looks like she should be in the army or something. She marches towards us and then freezes when she spots Picasso. He chooses this second to let us know how much he is enjoying his day by breaking into his howly happy song. His yaps make me wince.

'There's a *dog* in that bed,' states Uncaring in a disgusted voice. *Ten out of ten for observation*, I think, but I manage not to say it. I do have *some* self-preservation.

She turns to Beatrice and looks at her accusingly.

'Did you know about this?'

Beatrice looks back at her. She seems outwardly calm but I can feel her dislike for Uncaring radiating out from her. Picasso obviously feels the same way because he stands up and starts barking. Like, properly barking. Really loud, obnoxious, *I-don't-like-you* barking.

'I was dealing with it,' Beatrice tells her. She has to shout over the noise that Picasso is making. 'They're just leaving.'

'Oh no,' says Uncaring, scowling at us all. She even scowls at Martha, who glares back at her. 'They aren't going anywhere until I've called Mrs Thompson in here. This is a situation for senior management. And their parents too. This is an atrocious disregard for our rules and regulations. I said that we shouldn't allow young people in here in the first place.'

She turns to me. 'Where is your mother, young lady? I need to speak to her.'

'Good luck with that,' I mutter. 'She left eighty-five days ago.'

'Erin,' says Beatrice, a warning in her voice.

I stare down at my shoes. 'My dad is out in the garden,' I tell her.

'Oh – you're the *gardener*'s daughter,' says Uncaring. I don't like the way she spits it out, as if being a gardener's daughter somehow explains my shabby behaviour. I take a step forward but then Frog reaches down and takes hold of my hand, pulling me back to stand next to him. A buzz of something unexpected tingles in my hand as I feel Frog's fingers tighten round mine but there's no time to think about that because a crash from behind makes us all jump and we turn to the bed where Martha is struggling to sit up, her right hand still on the bedside table where she has slammed it.

She leans against the pillows and points her finger, first at Picasso and then at herself. Her hand is shaking but I think that right now that's down to anger, not old age.

Uncaring narrows her eyes and looks at Martha.

'Are you saying this is your dog?' she says.

Martha nods, glaring at Uncaring.

'That *is* interesting.' Uncaring turns to look at Beatrice. 'You are witness to the fact that she just admitted responsibility. She deliberately allowed a dog into a no-animals environment with no regard for the health and safety of the other residents.'

'Oh for goodness' sake –' starts Beatrice, but Uncaring interrupts her.

'Is that what you're saying? You are responsible for the presence of this dog?'

Martha nods and I am shocked by the look of triumph on Uncaring's face. I clench my fist but then Frog squeezes my hand and when I look at him he nods across to Martha.

She is smiling at me. And as I start to smile back I see her lips move. There is no sound but there doesn't need to be. It's easy to lip-read the 'thank you' that she mouths at me across the room. It's easy to see the sparkle in her eyes as Uncaring insists on going to fetch the manager and leaves the room, instructing Beatrice to make sure we don't escape, like she's the Child Catcher or something.

My amazing plan worked. And this makes it easier to cope when Dad is dragged in from the garden and Picasso and I are presented to him, along with instructions to 'take them both home right away'. It makes it easier to grip Frog's hand while his mum tells him that he should have known better and that she is 'disappointed' in him. All of these things are easy because we saved Martha from feeling like she had nothing to live for.

And I would do it all again tomorrow if I had to.

LAST SICKNESS*

I have had the best idea for our Martha Challenge EVER (or since the last time I had the best idea ever, anyway). Dad wasn't as cross as I thought he'd be about the whole Picasso/Oak Hill thing. In fact, I got the feeling that he thought it had been quite a good idea, even though he'd never actually say that to me. He gave me a hug when we'd got Picasso back into the van and told me

---

* *Last Sickness* (1953) by Alice Neel. There is something about this oil painting that makes me utterly sad. I'm not sure if it's the way that the old lady is slumped in her chair or if it's the fact that her glasses are all wonky, but she looks like she's really tired. And not the sort of tired that a good night's sleep will sort out but the sort of tired where she just might not bother to wake up in the morning. Alice Neel painted this picture of her mum and I think it looks like there's no life left in her. Like she's already gone.

that some care homes actually encourage people to bring animals in, that pet therapy can help people in all kinds of ways. That totally makes sense to me – Picasso always cheers me up if I'm feeling rubbish. Anyway, I'm allowed back at Oak Hill as long as I promise faithfully not to smuggle any animals of any kind in ever again. So I needed a plan that would help Martha without getting me into trouble.

She's much better than she was last week. I think the worst might be over now. When I went to see her a few days ago she was sitting up in bed, and yesterday she was actually in the day room. I've decided that we need to focus again on helping her move forward. On getting her living properly again. And I've got an idea that should do just that, as well as solving a problem of my own.

I haven't been able to get my iPad out of the box since my birthday two weeks ago. The guilty feeling I get when I even just look at it is horrible. And what makes it worse is that I know I'm really confusing Dad. He thought I'd be overjoyed to get it back – and I know it was really generous of him and Mum (he told me that Mum gave him half of the money that I stole from him when I bought it in the first place).

So my plan for today is doubly brilliant.

Dad looks a bit surprised and dubious when I get into the car carrying the iPad.

'Are you sure that's a good idea, love?' he asks me. 'You don't want it to go missing or get broken.'

'I'll take really good care of it,' I promise him. He HAS to let me take it to Oak Hill today. Now I've thought about this properly I can't wait any longer to carry out my plan.

'Well, if you're sure,' he says, reversing out of the drive.

The second we arrive I leap out of the van.

'See you later, Dad!' I call to him and then I walk as quickly as I can towards my secret hideaway. The day is hotting up already but it's starting to feel different. Like I can smell school in the air. It reminds me that I haven't got much time to help Martha before I'll be back in that place.

I'm so focused on the iPad that I don't even hear Frog approaching until he sits down next to me.

'Cool!' he says, reaching out to take it off me. 'I didn't know you had one of these. Give me a go!'

'No!' I say, pushing his hand away. 'It's not for you. It's for Martha.'

'OK.' Frog looks at me. 'What's she supposed to do with it, then?'

For a split second I consider not telling him. Just making it MY thing. But then I remember how generous he was with the Wii and a picture of him wiping Martha's chin pops into my head and I know that this will be far more fun with Frog than without him.

So I show him what I've found. And his mouth drops open and his eyes light up and when he looks at me I feel like he is REALLY looking at me, in a way that makes my face feel a bit hot.

'That is properly brilliant, Erin,' he tells me.

'I know, right?' I could pretend to be modest but I won't pull it off so there's no point. It IS properly brilliant!

'Shall we go and find Martha now?' he asks. I nod and together we walk down the path.

It's easy to track her down. She's in the dayroom with Frog's grandad playing on the Wii.

They're playing baseball, which from the sounds of it, is a bit of an extreme activity. I can hear Frog's grandad laughing before we even open the door and I'm glad that Martha has made a friend. It'll be good for her when Frog and I are back at school and can only visit at weekends.

'Hi, Grandad,' calls Frog, going over to give him a hug. 'How's it going?'

'Well, apart from not understanding the rules of this ridiculous game, I'm very well,' his grandad says, winking at me. 'Martha, my dear, shall we go back to the more civilized sport of tennis?'

'Sorry, Grandad,' says Frog. 'Erin needs to borrow Martha for a bit. She's got another plan.'

Martha looks at me and raises her eyebrows.

'You'll love it,' I tell her. 'I promise.'

'Oh well, another time, then,' says Grandad. Then he calls across the room to a lady who is snoozing in a chair. 'Hey, Doris! Fancy a quick round of golf before Beatrice brings the tea trolley in?'

I push Martha out of the room, Frog following behind us. When we're in the corridor I lean round the chair.

'Are you OK if we go for a walk?' I ask her. She nods, so Frog pushes open the side door and I carefully manoeuvre her on to the path. We've decided to take Martha to our secret hideaway. That way we won't be disturbed by anyone.

It turns out that pushing a wheelchair for any kind of distance on a gravel path is actually quite tricky. We take it in turns but still, I'm sweating and puffing and panting by the time we make it through the trees. The last part is super-difficult and I'm grateful that it hasn't rained for a while, otherwise the wheels would just sink straight into the grass. I know Uncaring said that Martha could walk if she wanted to, but I think that was just her being a cow. Martha's old. Her legs are probably really tired.

By the time we get to our bench I am exhausted, but I'm too excited to wait any longer. I've been carrying the iPad in my rucksack and I pull it out now and put it on Martha's lap.

She looks at it in confusion.

'This is going to help you talk again,' I tell her. 'Look.'

And then I turn it on and open the app that I bought with some of my savings. I get to the right page and start to explain, pointing out the buttons on the screen that need to be pressed.

'I've customized some of them to make them more personal, but there's loads of words already downloaded and if you want anything else we can create it ourselves. Look – I even added Picasso,' I tell her. 'You have a go.'

But Martha just sits, staring at the screen, looking as if she hasn't got a clue what I'm talking about.

I look in desperation at Frog. This HAS to work. Why isn't she trying it?

With his freaky mind-reading powers he answers my question.

'Show her again,' he whispers. So I do.

I show her how to swipe the pages to find different categories. I find the animal page and show her the button for 'frog'. I find the basic communication page and show her how to build a sentence. I show her everything and she doesn't make a single sound. She doesn't even twitch. She just sits, looking at the screen.

Eventually I get up and walk a few steps towards the stream. Frog follows me and puts his hand on my shoulder. He can tell I'm upset.

'She hates it,' I whisper, trying not to cry.

'I'm sure she doesn't,' Frog says but his voice isn't convincing.

I sigh and look up at the sky. There are more clouds now and there's a bit of a chill in the air. I hug myself, rubbing my hands up and down my arms. This is not at all how I thought it would be.

'We should probably get her back to the house before it rains,' I tell Frog. I feel completely miserable and for some reason, I wouldn't mind sharing a flask of tea with my dad right now.

'I guess,' says Frog. 'And then we can figure out something new to do with Martha. A new challenge.'

I haven't got anything to say to that. How can I tell him that I'm done? I'm out of ideas. I was so sure that this would work. My failure to improve Martha's life feels like a bad head cold – it's filling up my mind and making me feel stuffy and tired.

'Maybe she's too old for new technology,' I mutter. 'You know – that saying about how you can't teach an old dog new tricks.'

'I don't know,' says Frog thoughtfully. 'She handled the Wii pretty well.'

'Yeah, OK, no need to gloat,' I snap, without turning to look at him. 'Why don't you just say it – I'm never going to work out how to make her better.'

'Erin, it's not about making her better,' starts Frog. 'I think you should know that I was talking about Martha with my mum the other day and she told me that –'

But before he can tell me whatever it was his mum told him, we are interrupted by a sound. No, actually by a voice. A robotic voice that I'm sure sounds nothing like Martha's real voice, but a voice all the same.

'*I like Picasso.*'

We spin round and gape at Martha. She is sitting up very straight in her chair, iPad on her lap and smiling the biggest smile that I have ever seen. I walk over to her and stand, looking down at the iPad.

'Can you do it again?' I ask her, holding my breath. Frog is next to me and I grab his hand, squeezing it tightly. I wouldn't normally be so brave but I need the moral support right now. I really think this idea might work!

Martha bends her head over the iPad so that I can't see what she's doing. Then she sits up and touches the screen. The iPad speaks to us.

'*Thank you, Erin.*'

And I burst into tears. Which is highly embarrassing, especially as Frog doesn't let go of my hand, so I can't reach for a tissue and end up having to wipe my face with my sleeve.

Martha moves her fingers slowly across the iPad and I've started to get a grip when the next sentence arrives.

'*No cry face*,' she makes the robot voice say, which makes me cry a little bit more.

When I've stopped being lame we sit with Martha for half an hour, talking. It is the best thirty minutes of my life. Martha gets the hang of the communication app really quickly for such an old person and by the time we realize that the sky is getting dark, she's told us that her favourite food is trifle, she loves the rain and she wants us to keep practising the jitterbug.

The first raindrop splashes on to the iPad screen and I hurriedly grab it off Martha's knee and ram it into my rucksack.

'You might love the rain,' I tell her as Frog and I both take a wheelchair handle and shove her across the grass with all our strength, 'but Beatrice will not love us if we take you back soaking wet!'

And as the sky opens and chucks its contents down on to our heads, we race down the path, Martha shaking with laughter and Frog whooping like some kind of demented cowboy, and me feeling like I'm part of something important and special that will last forever.

Four days later I am sitting by the water fountain. It's just Martha and me today – Frog's mum insisted on taking him for a haircut and to buy new school uniform.

'I don't even want to think about this summer being over,' I tell Martha, plucking a blade of grass and trying for the millionth time to make that whistling sound that Frog's so good at. 'It'll be horrible thinking of you here on your own all day.'

'*I am lucky*,' Martha says. Well, obviously the iPad says it but she's getting quite speedy at selecting her sentences and we've programmed in loads of extra words so she can pretty much talk about anything.

'Yes, but it won't be the same when we can only come over at weekends,' I say.

I've been thinking about this a lot. It's not just Martha I'm going to miss when September starts. I can't seem to stop thinking about Frog when we're not together and he's always so friendly and funny but I have no idea if he likes me in the way I'm starting to like him. And he's in the year above me at school so I'm barely going to even see him during the week.

'I thought this summer was going to be rubbish,' I say. Martha grins. 'But it *hasn't* been,' I rush to tell her. 'Things have changed since that first week. Me and Dad are getting on quite well now and I can kind of see that him and Mum are better off apart.'

I saw Mum yesterday. I hadn't been sure about going but Martha persuaded me. Well, she didn't exactly persuade me because that suggests that there was a certain degree of discussion about the whole thing. Which there was not. I mentioned that I hadn't seen Mum for a few weeks but that she wouldn't stop ringing the house now that she's back from her holiday, and that she wanted me to go for tea with her and Mark and the mother-stealing children. Martha wrote a message in her notepad and wouldn't stop waving it at me until I eventually caved in and agreed to go just to shut her up. Her note was simple.

YOUR MUM LOVES YOU. NEW BEGINNINGS.

And it wasn't that bad, actually. Dad dropped me off and as soon as Mum opened the door she pulled me into a huge hug that felt really good. And Mark was OK, I suppose. He didn't try and act like my dad, which is a good job because I'd have definitely told him where to go if he'd tried that. The kids were pretty sweet. Annoying and noisy, but sweet. I ended up feeling bad that they didn't have a mum. I mean, my mum might not live in my house but at least she's alive. At least I can talk to her if I want to.

Dad was in a great mood when I got home and we stayed up late, watching a film and eating popcorn with Picasso snuggled up next to us on the sofa and trying to sneak popcorn when he thought we weren't looking. Dad was singing this morning when I got downstairs for breakfast. I think we're going to be OK.

'Anyway,' I tell Martha. 'It'll be no time really until October half-term and after that we've got two weeks off for Christmas. Then it'll be next year and before you know it we'll be nearly at the summer holidays and we can all be together for the whole six weeks!'

Martha is smiling as she chooses her words.

'*Don't wish time away,*' she tells me.

'I'm not!' I say. 'I'm just thinking ahead. We should make plans for next summer – really get out and do some stuff. We could take you for days out – maybe the beach, or shopping. What d'you reckon?'

I look at Martha to get her reaction. I know it might sound weird – after all, she's totally ancient and I didn't even know her at the start of the holidays – but I feel like she's almost family now.

Like she matters. I want to make sure that we don't all drift apart just because of something rubbish like school and I'm sure that Martha will be pleased I'm making plans for our time together.

But she isn't smiling any more. She's looking at me with a worried expression on her face, and when she puts the iPad to one side so that she can write her reply in her notepad, it seems to take her longer than normal to choose the right words. The iPad is brilliant but sometimes Martha still finds it easier to write things down, even though her hand is all shaky.

Finally she sits up and shows me what she's written.

NOBODY WILL TELL YOU WHEN IT'S YOUR LAST SUMMER AND YOU PROBABLY WON'T EVEN KNOW IT.

I frown at her.

'What does that even mean?'

She underlines the first part of her message.

NOBODY WILL TELL YOU WHEN IT'S YOUR LAST SUMMER.

I don't understand what Martha is trying to tell me. How can this possibly be my last summer?

She must be able to see my confusion because she turns to a fresh page and writes again.

THINGS CHANGE. YOU ARE CHANGING. I AM
CHANGING. GROWING OLDER.

'Oh, I get it,' I say. 'Yeah – things ARE different now to how they were before.' I grin at her, feeling a bit sheepish. 'I was a bit of a cow at the start of the summer, wasn't I?'

Martha shakes her head but she's smiling at me.

'I was completely childish about Mum and Dad splitting up. I acted like a right brat. I wasn't that great to you, either.'

Martha is furiously writing so I pause to give her time.

YOU'LL BE ALL RIGHT.

I think for a moment. 'Of course I will. And so will you. But you're right – I'm getting older. This is my last summer of being a kid. Next year I'm going to be utterly responsible and mature and Beatrice will let me and Frog take you out and we'll have a brilliant time!'

Martha looks tired and I stand up.

'Time to take you back for your rest,' I tell her. I pack away the iPad and start pushing her towards the house.

Afterwards, sitting behind Dad's shed with the sun on my face, I replay our conversation in my head. And I can't help feeling that Martha was talking about something else. That maybe it isn't just *my* last summer. There's a prickling sensation on the back of my neck and I shake it away. She shouldn't talk like that. Sure, we're all getting older, every single day but there's no point thinking about it. Not while there's still us. Not while there's still life.

MARTHA

Two strikes. They debated for a long time about whether the incident with the dog was serious enough to merit evicting me there and then, but eventually they decided that they would prefer to prolong the agony and keep me a little while longer. I suspect Beatrice was fighting my corner, arguing that I meant no harm. She really shouldn't have wasted her time.

I was actually feeling very low that day. I'd been thinking more and more about Tommy and Mim and those summer days that I thought would never end. I didn't think that Erin had it in her to genuinely surprise me but I must admit, when I saw that ridiculous dog standing next to me I was impressed. She's got something about her, that girl. I think she'll do well in life, as long as all her spirit and attitude isn't ground out of her, by those who think they know best.

This has not been a summer that I could have predicted. I have grown quite fond of Erin and Frog. The boy means well and has a good heart but he is not the one for Erin. Not like Tommy and I. The pair of us were well matched. We could have had a happy life together. Frog isn't strong enough to deal with Erin. He'll be much happier with someone good-natured like him. She has a darkness that needs to be dealt with by someone who feels it too. Someone who understands.

The summer is nearly at an end. I've been wondering about *lasts* and *ends* for some time now. When was the last time I rode a bicycle? When was the last time I tied my hair up in a ponytail? Who was the last person to give me a hug? There is a fact – when you do something for the last time you will probably have no idea of the significance. You will have no idea that this is the last time you will eat chocolate or the last time you will listen to music. You are blissfully unaware that this is the last train journey you will ever go on or the last book you will ever read. In fact, the last book you read may be one you dislike. It almost definitely will not be your favourite book.

Do not think, for one second, that these *lasts* only exist when you are old. They start creeping up on you. When I was thirty-five years old I realized that I had done my last handstand. I couldn't tell you when I did it but all I knew was that I could no longer perform a handstand if my very life depended upon it. My last handstand had happened.

I don't remember the last word that I spoke with my own, normal voice. I expect it wasn't important at the time. It feels quite important now, though.

I do remember my last summer, however. The months after Tommy had gone were the longest months of my life. Every day I waited for news and every day I was disappointed. I took to wearing the wedding ring he had given me, despite my parents' disapproval, and I bitterly regretted the way I had left him in the woods. I vowed to wait for him for as long as it took and I promised myself that when he returned I would never again leave him alone.

It was a beautiful sunny day when the news came. I remember vividly how the sky was the kind of blue that you see in paintings. It was almost too perfect to be real. I was sitting on the front step, peeling potatoes, and when my mother came down the street I could tell immediately that something was wrong. She stood in front of me and spoke the words and I looked over her shoulder at the sun and was amazed that it wasn't turning red. How could it continue to shine on a world where Tommy was no more? On a world that let living boys go to war and return as dead men?

Nothing was ever the same after that. Summer never felt like proper summer. But I kept my promise. I have continued to wait for Tommy, even though it has ended up taking a lifetime. My lifetime.

It's time to go. The children will be gone, back to their real lives and it's time for the ending. My ending. And, partly thanks to them, it's going to be a happy ending after all, despite what I've always imagined. This summer has brought a surprising end to many lonely years and I am alone no longer. I'm sure she'll never know it, but Erin has helped me to get better. A good death is as important as a good life and I am ready.

IN THE GARDEN*

'Pass me another sandwich,' I tell Frog, stuffing the last bits of crust into my mouth.

'Yes, your royal highness.' He salutes me and then chucks a ham sandwich across to me.

'Hey!' I protest, scrambling to catch it before it falls on the rug. 'Didn't your mother teach you anything about presentation?'

---

* *In the Garden* (1885) by Pierre-Auguste Renoir. The two people in this painting are sitting in a garden and I think they're in love. The thing is, the man is gazing at the lady as if she's the most interesting thing he's ever seen but she isn't looking at him. She's looking at us. And it's impossible to tell what she is thinking. Maybe she's imagining spending the rest of her life with him. Or perhaps she thinks it all seems a bit scary and she wishes that she was somewhere else.

He smirks at me and starts peeling an orange. I lean back on my elbows and look around. I'm hungry, but not for the amazing picnic that Frog's mum has packed for us. What I'm craving is memories. I'm desperate to store up everything that's happened this summer, because school starts tomorrow and it's going to suck.

Our secret hideaway looks even better than it did the first time I stumbled into it. The grass is full of cornflowers and daisies and it's grown really long. Sitting here we are hidden from view. Nobody would know we're here unless we wanted them to find us. Which we don't. I wonder for a few minutes if we could hide out in the gardens of Oak Hill and avoid going back to school. Delay September for just a few days. I'm not ready to give all of this up yet – Martha is using the iPad every day and getting faster and faster. It's almost like having a normal conversation with her now.

She hasn't mentioned anything about the past for ages. I think it's because she doesn't need the memories to feel happy. I think it's because Frog and I are making her happy. We're making her better. Giving her a reason to live.

She did give me that same message again the other day, though. She wrote it on a piece of paper and made me take it with me.

NOBODY WILL TELL YOU WHEN IT'S YOUR LAST SUMMER. ENJOY THE NOW, PERIN. LIVE FOR THE *NOW*.

It's all very well telling me to live for the now, but Martha isn't looking at spending the next eight weeks trapped in a smelly classroom, listening to Lauren and Nat witter on about their fascinating love lives with only algebraic fractions to distract me. That's if they'll even talk to me at all.

'Can I have a seggy?' I ask Frog.

He looks at me with pretend horror on his face. 'Can you have a *what*?'

'A seggy. You know – a segment of your orange.'

He frowns. 'I've just expended more energy on peeling this thing than I'm actually going to gain by eating it, you realize? You reckon I like you enough to share a piece of my hard-fought-for orange?'

'I know you do,' I tell him, stretching out my hand expectantly.

Frog passes me two segments of orange. 'It's true,' he sighs dramatically. 'I am powerless to resist your charms. In fact, is there anything else I can do for you while I'm here? Peel you a grape? Wash your stinky feet?'

He grabs my foot and starts to unlace my trainer. I shriek and thump his arm.

'Get off me, you weirdo! Don't go anywhere near my feet!'

'Ahh, I spot a weakness in your armour,' says Frog, but he lets go and lies down on the rug. 'Don't worry, your secret is safe with me. I won't tell a soul about your foul, fetid, feet.'

'FYI, I do NOT have smelly feet,' I tell him, trying to sound huffy but failing miserably. I lie down next to him and put my hands behind my head. 'Oh god, why do we have to go back to school tomorrow. I don't think I can cope.'

'You'll cope,' Frog says. 'You have to. Anyway, aren't you looking forward to seeing your friends?'

I groan. The thought of Lauren and Nat makes me feel even worse. I feel like I've changed a lot this summer and I just can't imagine spending my lunchtimes sitting on the wall and watching them snog whichever boy is flavour of the month.

Particularly when they always choose disgusting coffee flavour and I've got delicious mint choc chip right here next to me on this rug and I don't know how to tell him that I like him.

I really like him. A lot. I like him in that way where I always know where he is, even if I'm not looking right at him. I like him in the way that if he's nearby then all the hairs on my arm will stand up on end before we've even brushed against each other. I like him in the way that I miss him on the days we're not both at Oak Hill.

And after today it's all going to be over. Sure, we've promised that we'll visit Martha at weekends but I know he's got loads of friends. As soon as he's back at school he'll forget all about me. Frog's going to be in Year 10 and it's pretty much social death for any of them to talk to anyone in Year 9. And there'll be loads more homework for me and choosing my options for GCSEs and lots of other pointless activities that apparently are necessary if we are all to grow up.

And now it's our last afternoon. The last afternoon of summer and we can't decide what to do. Beatrice has brought Martha down to the water fountain and Frog and I are slumped on the bench, trying to agree on a fitting activity.

'We could practise the jitterbug,' suggests Frog. Martha looks keen but I shake my head.

'I am NOT in the mood for dancing,' I tell them.

'So what shall we do?' asks Frog. 'We don't want to waste the last afternoon.'

And that's the exact problem. It's too important a time to waste doing something rubbish – and nothing seems good enough.

'*A walk round the garden?*' types out Martha on the iPad, but I groan.

'Boring,' I tell her and then ignore her grimace. She hates me saying that. Last week she spent ages choosing the words in order to tell me that '*only boring people use the word boring*', which I told her was even more boring than the thing that had made me bored in the first place.

This is useless. I just want to spend the afternoon having fun with my two favourite people but we're all sitting here acting like we're at a funeral. If we don't decide on something soon then the afternoon will be gone.

I pick up my sketchpad from beside me and grab a pencil from my rucksack. I might as well do *something* until someone comes up with a plan. Without thinking about what I'm doing I start sketching Martha, using light pencil marks to outline her face.

After a few minutes I realize that Frog and Martha are watching me.

'Can I have a go?' asks Frog, and I tear a sheet of paper out of my pad and pass him a pencil. Then I carry on with my drawing. I've just got as far as Martha's nose when she thrusts a note at me.

AND ME?

I look up at Martha, unsure that I've understood her correctly. But she's smiling and pointing at my sketchpad, so I rip out another sheet and give her one of the art books that I've been lugging about for the last few weeks to lean on.

And then we sit quietly, the only sounds the scratching of the pencils. Frog is leaning over, resting his paper on the seat of the bench and glancing up at me every now and again. Martha is relaxed in her wheelchair and I'm pretty sure she's drawing Frog. I focus on my sketch and soon I am only aware of the picture, as I define the shape of Martha's face and shade and rework the marks I'm making until I can see her looking up at me from the page.

Eventually, Martha puts her pencil down and stretches in her chair. Frog stops fairly soon after and they talk to each other using the iPad while I finish. I don't want to rush – I can tell that this picture is going to be one of my best.

When I'm finished I look up. The last afternoon has gone. The sun is sinking fast and Martha looks like she feels cold.

'Where did the time go?' I ask.

Frog laughs. 'I guess we were all busy. Let's see your picture then!'

I'm suddenly a bit shy. 'No. you first. Come on – time to reveal your talents!'

'OK, you asked for it! Just remember that I did warn you about my lack of artistic ability.'

Frog spins his paper round to face us, with a big flourish.

'Ta da!' he says.

I was right. He has drawn a portrait of me. And he wasn't kidding, either – art is definitely NOT one of his strengths. And yet ... there's *something*. I take the picture from him and look at it closely. It looks nothing like me – the nose is too big and the chin is too square (at least I hope my chin doesn't look like that), but there's something about it that makes me feel good. Maybe it's the eyes. The me in the picture looks happy. She looks warm. She looks like the person who drew her really, really cares about her.

'I love it,' I tell Frog in a quiet voice. 'Can I keep it?'

'Yeah,' he says, and when I look up at him he looks me straight in the eyes and I see that his eyes are warm and happy and full of something special.

'Show us your drawing, Martha,' I say, forcing myself to look away from Frog before I say or do something utterly stupid.

Martha picks up her paper and passes it to Frog. I peer over his shoulder and stifle a laugh.

'Er . . . that's great?' he tells Martha hesitantly.

Martha smiles, which is good because I can't restrain the giggles that have been building up in my throat any longer. She has drawn a picture of a frog. And it's pretty awful. One eye is twice the size of the other and some of the lines zip right off the page.

'You can tell it's meant to be a frog, though,' I say, through my laughter. It's really important to be positive about other people's art – even when it's virtually impossible to find something to be positive about.

Martha smiles and wiggles her right hand at us.

I look at her in surprise. 'You used your right hand?'

She nods proudly.

'Martha! That's brilliant! I didn't know you could hold a pencil yet. You must have been doing your exercises then?'

She nods.

'In that case,' says Frog, 'this is an amazing piece of art. I shall treasure it forever!'

We laugh and I suddenly feel that we've spent the last afternoon doing something perfect.

'Your turn, Erin,' Frog tells me. 'Come on, you can't wriggle out of it any more. Show us what you've got.'

I get up and stand next to Martha.

'I did this for you,' I tell her. 'I wanted to show you what I see when I look at you.'

I put the paper down on her lap and wait. Martha looks down at the page and my drawing. I have drawn her, but not how she looks now. I've tried to look behind the wrinkly skin and the saggy eyes and the tired mouth. Instead I've

drawn the Martha who could do the jitterbug.
The Martha who loved No-good Tommy. I don't
know if I've got it right until she looks up at me,
tears streaming down her face.

'Don't cry!' I say, feeling alarmed. 'I didn't
mean to make you sad. I'm sorry!'

Martha wipes her eyes with her sleeve and
looks again at the picture, pointing first at it and
then at herself.

'You can keep it,' I tell her. 'Just no cry
face, OK?'

Martha leans over and grips my hand, her
grasp surprisingly firm. I can feel the bones
beneath the soft, wrinkly skin and I think that
this is what being old is all about. The same
person inside but barely recognizable to yourself
in the mirror. I think about how Martha isn't
bothered about rules and all the things she's
taught me this summer. I wonder if I'd have found
those things out for myself anyway or if I'd have
had to wait until I was an old lady to work out
what really matters. I wonder how much stuff we
don't get told before it's too late.

And that's it. The last afternoon has been and
gone. When I get into bed that night I prop up

Frog's picture against my bedside lamp, where I can see it as I fall asleep. I wonder if Martha has done the same thing with my drawing. The words she gave me are buzzing round my brain and even though I'm trying not to think about it I can't help knowing two things.

This was the last afternoon. And it was also the last summer.

FISH AND FROGS *

The first day back at school is as predictably awful as usual. Teachers prattling on about how much fun we're going to have this year and how, now that we're in Year 9, we'll be given extra responsibility and independence. Why do adults always go on about responsibility like it's a *good* thing? I'm more than happy to carry on doing what I've always done – which is sit at the back of the classroom, paying just enough attention to get by and counting down the hours until the final bell.

---

* *Fish and Frogs* (1949) by M. C. Escher. This is a brilliant picture where fish and frogs tessellate together and you're never really sure what you're meant to be looking at. One second you're sure that you're looking at a frog and then BOOM – it's gone. It's confusing. Everything changes in the blink of an eye.

Anyway, surprise, surprise, it's all lies. By the end of the first day it is obvious that nothing has changed. Lessons are the same boring lessons that they were last year. And that means that they are nobody's definition of fun. The only good part of the day was art when we had to hand in our summer projects. Miss Jenson flicked through them during the lesson and asked me to stay behind after class. I thought I was in trouble for a moment but then she said that she was really impressed with my enthusiasm and had I thought about doing art GCSE? I was a bit embarrassed but she started talking about the paintings I'd chosen and we ended up having a good chat. She gave me a spare art book to keep at home and said if I wanted to carry on the project then she'd love to see my ideas every now and again. I told her I'd think about it but I took the art book anyway. Just in case.

I don't see Frog until the second day. I'm walking into the cafeteria and suddenly there he is, right in front of me. He spots me at the exact same moment that I see him and we both stand still, looking at each other.

He looks different. And it isn't just the school uniform, although I guess that's part of it. He seems older and more distant and I suddenly feel awkward. I don't know what to say to him so I keep standing there. And then he's being shoved towards me by his group of friends who don't understand why he's suddenly stopped moving. They're confident and raucous and one of them says something to him as he goes to walk past me that makes them all laugh really loudly.

'Hi, Erin,' he says and raises his hand in a greeting but he doesn't stop to talk and for some reason I look away. I act like I don't hear him and make my legs move forward so that I'm rejoining the queue for food. I collect a tray and shuffle slowly forward, then collect a plate and ask for a baked potato and some fish fingers and then I shuffle forward a bit more and take a drink and pay at the till, and the entire time I manage not to glance over to the table where I know he's sitting. I think I can feel him watching me but I could be making it up. I don't know.

I'm ready for him on the third day and when I see him coming down the corridor I play it cool. I busy myself putting my books in my locker until I reckon he's almost next to me. Then I drop one of the books on the floor and bend down to pick it up. He almost walks right into me.

'Hey, watch it!' he says, and then he sees it's me. 'Erin!'

'Oh, hi,' I say, aiming for casual nonchalance but achieving jumpy nervousness. Frog laughs.

'Hi, yourself,' he says and grins at me in a way that makes me feel like nothing's changed.

'How's it going?' I ask him, still feeling a bit small and embarrassed. It seems so weird talking to him here, at school. Like our summer together never really happened.

'Oh, all as boring as usual,' Frog tells me, waving his hand dismissively in the air. 'We still on for Saturday?'

This is the real reason that I've been feeling odd. I was so sure that something would go wrong once we got back to school and that all the plans we made at Oak Hill would disappear, along with the summer. I thought that Frog wouldn't want anything to do with me when he was back with his mates. And Saturday will be One Hundred Days Without Mum and I really, really want to do something fantastic to distract me.

The relief makes me want to sit down.

'Absolutely!' I say, trying not to smile too enthusiastically. I don't want him to think I'm desperate to spend time with him. 'I'll see you there.'

We look at each other and for a second I think he's about to say something else. But then Lauren and Nat ruin it.

'Ooh, Erin! Introduce us to your new friend!' Nat is talking in a ridiculous, sing-song voice that makes me want to put my hand over her mouth.

I turn to glare at her and see Lauren gazing at Frog, her hands on her hips and her eyes open very wide. I happen to know that this is her seductive look and she practises it in front of the mirror.

'Hi,' she purrs. 'I'm Loz. I'm sure I've seen you on the football team.'

Frog smiles at her. 'No, not me. You must be thinking of someone else.'

'Oh, but you must be on one of the sports teams, surely?' Lauren is in full-blown attack mode and I need to get Frog out of here. Now. 'You look so sporty.'

Normally this kind of line would have me snorting in hilarity but today I'm not finding it very funny. I'm plotting the most painful, torturous punishment that I can think of to administer to my so-called best friend. How can she think it's acceptable to try to chat up MY – My brain freezes. My *what* exactly? What does Frog actually mean to me? More importantly, what do I mean to him? Maybe I have no right to be offended by Lauren's behaviour. After all, it's not like we're going out or anything. But he's totally not her type. His hair's a total state, for starters.

'Sorry,' says Frog to Lauren. 'You've got me totally wrong. I am the least active person you are ever likely to meet.'

As he turns to leave he gives me a wink and whispers, 'Saturday,' just loud enough for Lauren and Nat to hear. Then he's gone and I'm left to fend off the thousands of questions being fired at me by the girls.

'OMG, Erin! Is he your boyfriend?' screeches Nat.

'You kept him quiet,' says Lauren, sounding a bit annoyed. 'No wonder you weren't interested in Dom when you had *him* waiting for you.'

'It isn't like that,' I protest but the honest truth is that I don't *know* what it is like.

'Oh yeah?' Lauren isn't convinced. 'I don't know why you're keeping him such a big secret. Is he a bit odd or something?'

'I thought he seemed quite nice,' offers Nat and I smile gratefully at her.

Lauren exhales loudly. There is no physical reason for her to do this but it does a good job of conveying her frustration to the rest of us.

'I didn't say he wasn't *nice*, Nat,' she says in a slightly huffy voice. 'I'm sure he's perfectly *nice*. He's quite good-looking too, I suppose. He's just a bit immature, particularly when you compare him to Dom.'

'Oh god, no,' agrees Nat, keen to win back her best friend status with Lauren. 'He's nothing compared to Dom.'

'He obviously fancies you, though, Erin.' Lauren's voice is almost accusing and I wish she'd shut up. It's ridiculous to compare Frog to Dom – it's like trying to compare a pizza with a giraffe. They have no similarities so you can't figure out which one is better. They're just a pizza and a giraffe.

'Do you fancy him?' Nat is back to using the cutesy voice that she employs when she's talking about boys. For a second I want to ignore her but then I remember that she's my friend. That they're both my friends and that they have generously forgiven me for my antisocial behaviour at the barbecue party.

So I walk to science, trying to reply to their incessant questioning and wishing that I knew the answer to at least one of them.

LIFE DEATH, KNOWS
DOESN'T KNOW*

The only thing that has kept me going all week is the thought of going back to Oak Hill and the surprise that Frog and I have planned for Martha. It's Saturday morning and Dad nearly chokes on his cornflakes when I emerge into the kitchen, dressed and ready to go.

'Off somewhere?' he asks.

* *Life Death, Knows Doesn't Know* (1983) by Bruce Nauman. This art is made out of flickering neon lights that flash up different words: *Cares Doesn't Care, Knows Doesn't Know, Pleasure Pain Love Hate*. I feel like I don't know anything, definitely not what I'm supposed to be doing or how I'm supposed to be feeling. And I'm wondering how I can go from happiness to sadness so quickly.

'Gross, Dad,' I say, pulling out a chair and pouring myself some cereal. 'Don't talk with your mouth full!'

He swallows in an over-the-top, dramatic way and grins at me. 'Sorry, it was just the shock of seeing you up before lunchtime! I thought you'd be desperate for a lie-in today, especially when you knew I'd be doing overtime at Oak Hill.'

'I'm meeting Martha and Frog,' I tell him and he nods. That's the great thing about my dad. He doesn't feel the need to pry into every single thing that I do. He knows that I'm friends with Frog and that we've been spending loads of time with Martha but he never asks me about it. Mum wouldn't have stopped quizzing me about what I was getting up to and if Frog was my boyfriend. And as I don't exactly know the answer to that last question then I'm grateful that Dad just lets me get on. It feels like he's starting to trust me and I won't let him down again.

As soon as I've finished eating I grab my iPad and sketchbook and pack them into my rucksack. I wanted to leave the iPad with Martha but she wouldn't let me. She told me that it wouldn't be right but that she wouldn't mind borrowing it when I was visiting.

The drive to Oak Hill takes ages today. First we're stuck at a red traffic light for AGES and then we have to take a detour because there are roadworks or something. I beg Dad to drive as quickly as he can and by the time we pull up outside the house I'm feeling really impatient.

The second the van stops I open the door. I've got one foot outside on the gravel when Dad stops me.

'Erin,' he says, putting his hand on my shoulder.

'What?' I ask, reaching down for my bag.

'Just wait a second.' His voice sounds odd and I turn back to face him. He's not looking at me, although his hand has tightened its grip on my shoulder. I follow his gaze and stare out of the front windscreen.

Frog is standing on the steps to Oak Hill with his grandad. Beatrice is standing behind him and the look on her face makes my stomach flip over. I can't see Frog properly for a moment because his grandad has pulled him into a tight hug – but then he must realize that I'm there and he lifts his head.

Frog looks utterly miserable. He's obviously waiting for me because one hand is clutching a CD player and I wonder if we're ever going to actually need it now. I have a sudden memory of Frog gently wiping the water from Martha's chin with a tissue and I hope that one day, when he is old, someone will do the same thing for him.

'Erin,' starts Dad and I know. I know that it's happening all over again. It was just the same when Mum left. One day she was there and the next she was gone. Boom. A bit like a magic vanishing trick. It seems unfair – surely we'd be able to cope a bit better if someone gave us a bit of warning. It makes me wonder if there's something about me that makes people want to leave.

I get out of the van and look over at Frog. He says a few words to his grandad and then walks down the steps and across to where I'm standing.

'She's gone,' he tells me.

I don't know what this even means. Gone? Gone where? I know that I should be feeling scared or upset or something but I'm really not. I'm mostly feeling angry. We had a plan and now it's pointless, which pretty much makes the entire summer a waste of time.

'They've sent her away. Got rid of her.' Frog sounds angry too but I think his anger is for different reasons to mine.

'Now then, it's not quite like that.' Beatrice has followed Frog down the steps and is standing behind him.

'What is it like, then?' He rounds on her and she looks at him with a slightly surprised expression on her face. 'Because she's not here, is she? Grandad told me all about the stupid "three strikes and you're out" system.'

I look from one to the other. Beatrice looks upset and I think that Frog is getting cross with the wrong person. It isn't her fault. It wasn't her that chose to behave in a totally inappropriate way for an old person. There are rules. Martha knew what she was doing.

'Martha wasn't sent away because she did something wrong,' Beatrice tells us. 'It was just time for her to move on. She needed a different kind of care – more than we can give here at Oak Hill.'

'What do you mean?' asks Frog. 'What kind of care?'

Beatrice looks at us and I can see the kindness in her eyes. 'Martha is very old. She needs to be somewhere that can look after her and keep her out of pain for these last few weeks. She asked me to say goodbye to you both and to thank you for a wonderful last summer.'

I've heard quite enough. I turn round and I start walking across the car park and I ignore Dad calling me, and as soon as I reach the trees I start running. It feels good and I don't stop until I reach the secret hideaway. Then I collapse on to the grass and listen to my heart going crazy. I like it – it's hard to think of anything else when you believe you might actually be having a heart attack.

Eventually, though, my breathing slows down and the sounds of the real world float back in. I can hear the wind rustling in the trees and the stream trickling over the stones. And footsteps coming towards me and a voice calling my name.

I knew that he'd find me here. I wanted him to. He's the only person who can possibly know how I'm feeling right now.

The grass is so long that he almost treads on me, stopping just before he crushes my fingers under his foot. He sinks down beside me and reaches out for my hand and we lie on the slightly damp grass. We don't talk but I'm pretty sure we're thinking the same thoughts.

After a while, Frog sits up and pulls me with him.

'I can't believe she's gone,' he tells me. 'It's not going to be the same around here without her.'

'I wish we'd done more fun things with her,' I say. 'Really made the most of the summer. And I wish she'd cared enough about us to let us know that she was leaving. Given us a chance to say goodbye.'

And as I say it I remember Martha telling me, just last week, that we have to live in the now. That one summer will be our last summer. I thought that we had a lifetime of summers ahead of us but I was wrong.

We sit quietly for a while and then I think about something Frog said to Beatrice.

'What were you on about when you said, "three strikes and you're out"?' I ask him.

He sighs. 'Grandad told me. Apparently, Martha was on a warning. You know, like at school. She did something wrong and they said she had to leave. The first two things were to do with smoking and Picasso.'

I look at him guiltily. Does he mean the time I gave Martha a cigarette in the garden? And Picasso? That was totally my fault, not hers.

'What was the third thing?' I ask him, holding my breath and praying that it isn't something to do with me.

'Something to do with refusing her medication and telling Uncaring exactly what she thought of her. Grandad said she was a stubborn old woman who knew her own mind.'

'That figures,' I say, my guilty conscience making me feel annoyed. 'She was always on the lookout for trouble.'

And suddenly the absence of Martha hits me and the loss of her feels like a sharp kick in the ribs. No more reading her notes or telling her about my day. No more confiding in her about Mum. No more racing her wheelchair around the garden or seeing the look on her face when I sneak Picasso in to visit her. No more Martha. Ever.

'Stupid old people,' I mutter. 'Doing whatever they feel like and leaving us to pick up the pieces. Just like everybody else. Martha was only interested in herself all along.'

My crying is ugly. Normally I would hide it from Frog but today I can't. I'm gulping for air and my face feels red and I'm sure my nose has swollen to twice its normal size. My tears are hot and sticky and endless and I know that nobody on TV has ever cried in such an unattractive way as I do.

But Frog takes the two steps that separate us and holds me close. He doesn't seem to mind my snotty nose and shuddering body. He doesn't let go until I've calmed down and then we break apart and look at each other.

'You look a state,' he says, laughing a bit. 'Come on – no cry face.'

'Thanks very much,' I tell him, searching my pockets for a tissue.

'We could find out where she's been sent,' Frog tells me but his voice is hesitant and unsure.

I shake my head. If Martha had wanted to say goodbye to us then she'd have done it last week. And I guess she did, in her own way.

Frog turns towards the stream and starts scuffing his feet into the grass and suddenly I feel incredibly tired. I don't want to talk to anyone any more, not even Frog. I remember my pact not to speak when I first came to Oak Hill back at the start of the summer. Maybe I should have kept it. Maybe, if I hadn't ever spoken to Martha or Frog then I wouldn't be feeling like this now. I am so sick of feeling sad when people leave me. It'd be better for everyone if I just didn't bother getting to like them in the first place.

'I'm going home,' I tell him and I trudge towards the path, past the bench and under the trees. It doesn't seem like a safe, secret hideaway now. As the sun starts to disappear and the air gets chilly I know that time is running out for us, just like it ran out for Martha at Oak Hill. The movie credits will roll and there will be no happy ever after. My new beginning will finish before it even really began.

ME AND THE MOON*

The last few weeks have been seriously dull. Like, as if time is actually flatlining. I've been hanging around with Lauren and Nat again and it's like the summer never really happened. They've even convinced me to go to the cinema with them and, yes, Dom will be there too. They've told me that I should give him a break and that he really likes me. And that it makes everything easier if we can hang out in a big group.

* *Me and the Moon* (1937) by Arthur Dove. The colours at the top of this painting make it look beautiful and calm until you look down. Then you realize that the mood has changed and it feels sad and depressed. And then you notice that the moon has been broken and you're not sure that it can be fixed.

I've deliberately avoided Frog at school. It's not been that easy. I miss hanging out with him and talking about random stuff and coming up with crazy plans to help Martha. I even miss our stupid dance practices. But I need to be realistic. Nothing lasts forever, even if you really want it to. Frog belongs to the summer and the summer is long over. Martha and him are in the past. They're history.

Dad is totally doing my head in too. He's got loads of overtime work at the weekends and he keeps trying to convince me to go with him but I'm not interested. There's nothing at Oak Hill for me now.

I'm sitting in the front passenger seat of Dad's van. He's insisted that I need to come out with him tonight and I'm bored already. Autumn has really arrived and the streets are getting dark. As we drive down the road I can glance into the windows of the houses and get tiny, microsecond glimpses into the lives of the people inside. Here, a dark room only lit by the weird, flickering light that must be the television. And there, an old man who has paused midway through closing the curtains. He's peering out into the dark as if he's looking for something and I wonder who he's waiting for. He looks as if he might have been waiting for a long time.

I have no idea where we're going until Dad makes a left turn off the main road and we head away from town.

'Dad –' I say, but he doesn't let me continue.

'Just trust me, Erin, OK?' He looks over at me and puts his hand on my knee, giving it a quick squeeze. 'It'll be all right.'

I don't answer him because he knows that I didn't want to come here. But he brought me anyway. He probably thinks he knows what's best for me because he's the adult and I'm only thirteen. Nothing ever changes.

As the lights of Oak Hill flood the windscreen I feel myself getting moody. This is so boring and I was supposed to be meeting everyone in town in an hour. Lauren was not impressed when I phoned her to cancel. Dad stops the van and we sit in silence for a moment. Then he opens his door and gets out. When it's clear to him that I have no intention of moving, he bends down and pokes his head back into the van.

'You might as well get out now we're here,' he tells me. 'I've got a few jobs to do and there's no point you sitting out here in the cold.'

I open my door and get slowly out of the van. Dad has gone round to the back and opened up the double doors.

'You can give me a hand, actually, love,' he calls and I trudge across the gravel and round the side of the van.

The top half of Dad is hidden and as I watch he emerges, holding a bucket that has some gardening tools inside.

'I need you to take this down to the garden for me,' he says, passing the bucket to me.

'Now?' I ask him. It's getting pretty dark and I'm not in the mood for faffing about in the cold.

'Yes, please. It'll be one less thing for me to do on Monday morning.'

I raise my eyebrows at him to show that I am unimpressed.

'And then can we go home?' I ask.

'Yes,' he tells me. 'Right – I want this in that scrappy old bit of garden that's at the end of the path going past the water fountain. Beyond the hedge. I'm giving it a makeover – it's been completely neglected and I think it'd make a great relaxation area for some of the more mobile residents. Do you know where I mean?'

I nod. I DO know exactly where he means. My secret hideaway. The last place on earth that I want to go right now.

'*Dad*,' I whine, trying to look small and vulnerable. 'That's *miles* away. I don't like being in the dark on my own.'

Dad looks at me, his eyes suddenly piercing. 'Since when?' he asks. 'Look, Erin, I just need to do a few things and then we can get out of here. We could collect pizza on the way home if you like. What do you say?'

'OK,' I tell him grudgingly. 'Pizza *might* make up for the slave labour you're forcing upon me.'

'Good,' Dad says. He grabs his toolbox from the van and slams the doors. 'I'll meet you back here as soon as you're done.' And then he strides off towards the house, without so much as a backwards glance at me.

I sigh. Might as well get this over and done with. I get a better grip on the handle of the bucket and set out across the grass. Darkness is flooding in from all sides but there's a huge moon in the sky and it lights up the garden like a weird, galactic night light.

But when I walk under the trees it's as if someone has turned the moon off. The branches overhead block out any light and I stumble over twigs and stones that in the daytime wouldn't cause me any trouble. It feels wrong out here on my own and even though I was lying when I told Dad that I was afraid of the dark, I'm starting to feel a little bit freaked out.

The end of the path is in sight now and I can see a faint glow ahead of me. I speed up and by the time I emerge from the tunnel of trees I am virtually running.

And then I'm not running any more. I'm standing totally still, unable to move or speak or even think straight. My brain is trying to make sense of the scene in front of me and failing miserably. I have no idea what I'm looking at, just that it is beautiful.

The glow wasn't coming from the moon. It was coming from the hundreds of fairy lights that are strung over the hedges and lower branches of the trees. Lanterns are hanging down from some of the higher branches and as the wind picks up, they sway, casting their brilliant warmth across the long grass.

And it isn't just the light. It's the sounds. Tinkling, jingling, ringing sounds that are being made by the wind chimes that share the branches with the lanterns. I step closer and see that the chimes are all different. One is made using forks and spoons. Another with odd metal bits and pieces that look like the contents of Dad's toolbox – washers and bits of pipe and a spanner. This one (and it's definitely my favourite) has lots of dangling keys, all different shapes and sizes.

Another sound drifts towards me, carried by the wind that is getting stronger. I turn and peer into the darkness but before I can move a figure moves forward out of the gloom.

'Did you do this?' I ask him, although I think I already know the answer.

'With a lot of help from your dad,' he tells me. 'I told him that I was missing you and that we had a plan that needed to be finished.'

'Why?' I whisper.

'You know why,' he says. 'We're not done yet.'

I didn't want this. The summer is over. Martha's gone and we're back at school and everything is the same as it was before. Nothing has changed and it's crazy to think that this summer meant anything.

But then I look at Frog and I know that I'm not quite telling myself the whole truth. Some things *have* changed. I drop the bucket on the ground and walk across to him. I wrap one arm round his shoulder and we stand side by side, part of me amazed at how right it feels to touch him. How he makes me feel alive.

'I don't know what we're supposed to do now,' I say without looking at him. 'I don't know how we're supposed to be feeling.'

He thinks for a minute and I'm glad that he doesn't just give me a rehearsed answer. I like that he actually stops and thinks about it.

'I think we can feel anything we want,' he tells me.

THE DANCE OF LIFE *

We stand for a while and I think about what Frog has said. We can feel anything we want to. Is he right? I have no idea. I just know that I usually get it wrong and when it comes to thinking about how I feel about Martha leaving and how I feel about Frog being here right now, I don't even know where to begin.

* *The Dance of Life* (1900) by Edvard Munch. This painting shows three women at different stages of life. The woman in a white dress on the left is waiting for it to be her time to dance. The woman in the red dress in the middle is dancing with her partner, ignoring everyone else around her. The woman in the black dress on the right has had her dance and all she can do now is watch and remember. This picture makes me think that we should dance while it's our turn, because one day we'll be the ones who are watching and the only thing left will be our memories.

Eventually Frog pulls away from me.

'I've got something to show you,' he tells me. 'Close your eyes.'

'Frog!' I protest, as he moves behind me and covers my eyes with his hands. 'It's pitch-black out here! I can't see a thing as it is.'

'Just keep them closed and walk,' he says and then he nudges me in the back of the knee, forcing me to take a step.

I stretch my arms out in front of me. 'If you let me bump into something,' I warn him, 'I'll be seriously narked off with you.'

'Yeah, yeah, whatever,' he says and I can hear that he's enjoying himself.

'Like to live dangerously, don't you?' I mutter, taking tiny steps and trying to visualize where we're going.

Then we stop and Frog removes his hands and I open my eyes and blink. There, standing in front of me, is the most amazing thing I have ever seen. Even for Dad, this is good. It's more than good.

'It's perfect,' I breathe.

'I think it looks like Martha,' says Frog, and the sound of his smile makes me feel warm and lit up.

It's a dancer. Dad has used willow canes to create a flowing sculpture that almost looks like it's been made out of liquid. Her head is thrown back and one of her arms stretches out behind her while the other reaches up to the sky. She looks passionate and proud and completely at one with the earth.

'Your dad says that if we keep it watered then it'll probably grow leaves in the spring,' Frog tells me. 'It's a living willow sculpture. It should keep on growing every year.'

I can't tear my eyes away from the dancing Martha. Her body is full of life.

'I'm ready.' I turn to Frog and take his hand. 'This is perfect.' And as the words come out of my mouth I realize that I actually mean them. Here *is* perfect and our plan is perfect and we can do this.

We walk through the dark, Frog leading me to a circle of mown grass that I hadn't noticed before.

'What about music?' I ask him. 'There's no plug socket out here.'

'Batteries,' he says. He bends down and shows me his CD player, sitting on a bit of wood to keep it safe. Taking off my jacket I walk over to the bench and lay it over the top. When I turn back I see Frog, standing in the middle of the circle, waiting for me. For a moment he's frozen and I think that this is a memory that I would like to keep forever. The fairy lights and the lanterns and Frog. Then he presses 'play' and I run across to where he's standing on the grass.

We both spent weeks practising in the summer. The plan was to surprise Martha with an actual performance, and that kind of didn't work out, but I don't think that matters now. Anyway, our hard work has paid off because as the music blares out across the darkening sky, we spin and kick and twirl – all without falling over once. And we're dancing not just for Martha but for the summer and for us.

As Frog spins me towards him for our grand finale I imagine Martha, sitting in her wheelchair and clapping. I dip down towards the grass, my head thrown back and I look up at the sky. I'm dancing. And I'm not actually as awful as I thought I'd be.

Frog pulls me back up and my face is suddenly inches away from his. I can see his eyes, staring, and it looks like he's just seen something wonderful so I try to twist my head to look behind me. I want to see what he's looking at.

But he brings his hands up and holds on to my face and I have another moment of knowing. He's looking at *me*. The music must have stopped – either that or the insane beating of my heart is drowning out all other sounds. And as Frog brings his lips towards mine I think of what I want to tell Martha right now.

I want to tell her that I understand. That growing older doesn't mean having to grow up. I want to tell her that I have just said goodbye to finding a happy ending and hello to a new beginning. I want her to know that I danced and I truly didn't care if I was good or bad – I just got up and danced anyway.

And as Frog and I kiss each other I know two things. The first is that I will always be glad that my very first kiss was mint choc chip. And the second is that this IS my last summer. *Everything* has changed. Martha and Frog and this kiss mark the start of a whole lot of new, different types of summer. I will never again be the person I was before Frog kissed me. This feels like an OK thing.

THE PHYSICAL
IMPOSSIBILITY OF
DEATH IN THE MIND
OF SOMEONE LIVING*

Here are four things that I know. They are things that Martha told me and they're things that it took her a lifetime to discover. Nobody told her

* *The Physical Impossibility of Death in the Mind of Someone Living* (1990) by Damien Hirst. This piece of art is actually a dead tiger shark, floating in a tank of formaldehyde, which means it won't go rotten for years. Lots of people got a bit upset about this piece of art. Some people said it wasn't even art and that it was rubbish. Damien Hirst was cool, though – when someone told him that anyone could have done that with a shark and called it art, he just said 'But they didn't, did they?' I actually think it's OK. I think it shows how difficult it is for humans to think about dying. And maybe, it means that something isn't really dead if it still exists in the minds of the people left alive. I like that idea a lot.

288

this stuff, but she told me so that I wouldn't waste a single minute more.

1. You have to grow old. That's kind of obvious. Nobody can stop time and people age – even people who fight against it and get all sorts of freaky plastic surgery. They're still getting older on the inside, every day. But you don't have to grow up. Nobody can force you to be sensible or mature if you don't want to be. And when you're old, you'll still be *you*. Just a bit more wrinkly and tired, that's all.

2. If you can't find a happy ending then look for a new beginning. It's OK to start again – people do it every day. We shouldn't waste our energy trying to fix a situation that can't be fixed. And you never know, the new beginning might end up leading you to a better story anyway.

3. Nobody cares if you are totally and utterly rubbish at dancing. You should just get on your feet and dance. I'm glad I've not had to wait until I'm an old lady to learn this one, otherwise I'd have spent my entire life not dancing. Now I can do a pretty passable jitterbug, even if I do say so myself.

4. Nobody will tell you when you'll have your last summer and there's a good chance that you won't even know it. My summers will never be the same again – I know that I've had my last true summer as a kid. I need to do what Martha told me and live for the now. And I think that maybe Martha knew this was her last summer and she spent it doing exactly what she wanted to do.

Martha taught me these four things over the summer and I know I'll never forget her, not even when I'm an old lady and probably have no memory of what I had for breakfast.

I had to wait for the fifth thing she taught me until three weeks after she left.

The sound of the postman dropping the letters through the door makes me look up. Every so often Frog writes me a letter. It's silly really. We see each other most days at school and hang out together at the weekends – but still, his letters make me feel like the most important person in the world. Like I'm somebody worth spending time thinking about.

I was worried that nothing would be the same after Oak Hill, that the magic of our time together might have ended when normal life kicked in. And it isn't the same. It's better. I've still got my amazing memories of the summer and they feel really special – but I'm mostly enjoying the NOW, not living in the past.

I leave my sketchpad on the kitchen table and head out into the hall. There's quite a lot of post and I sift through quickly, putting most of it in a pile for Dad to deal with. The last envelope is addressed to me, though.

I can tell straight away it isn't from him. It's not written in a young person's handwriting. Tearing it open I reach inside and pull out a compliment slip with the Oak Hill logo on the top. I pause for a moment, suddenly reluctant to read the message. What if it's bad news? I haven't heard anything about Martha since the day that she left – it's like she's disappeared off the face of the planet – but it's in the back of my mind that she was old and ill. One of these days is going to be her last day and I'll never know.

Dear Erin,

I hope this finds you well. I came across this when I was sorting through some paperwork. Martha asked me to pass it on to you — my apologies for not posting it sooner. I hope we'll see you at Oak Hill with your dad sometime soon.

Best wishes,
Beatrice x

Inside the envelope is a single sheet of A4 paper. I ease it out carefully and recognize it instantly. It's the picture I did of Martha, back on our last afternoon of the summer. And at the bottom is a message. I can tell that Martha wrote it with her right hand because the handwriting is all wobbly and spidery. I read the words that probably took her ages to write.

The sketch is good. I know that sounds big-headed but it really is. Martha looks happy and vibrant and alive. I think that when I remember her, I'm going to remember this Martha, because that's who she really was. Her tired, frail body slowed her down but in her head she was young.

I look again at her message.

DEAREST ERIN,

OUR SUMMER TOGETHER IS OVER AND WE HAVE BOTH CHANGED, IN MANY DIFFERENT WAYS. I HAVE HAPPENED. BUT YOU ARE HAPPENING RIGHT NOW. THIS IS THE TRUTH AND I AM GLAD OF IT. REGRET NOTHING - LIVE IN THE MOMENT. AND THANK YOU FOR HELPING ME TO END WELL. IT MATTERED.

FONDEST LOVE,
MARTHA

X

I walk back into the kitchen and put the picture carefully on the table. I crouch down next to Picasso, who is fast asleep, and ruffle his fur. He's been sleeping a lot lately and Dad has started talking about his age and saying that, in dog years, he should be drawing his pension by now. I know what he's trying to tell me but I don't want to think about it too much. I just make sure that I give Picasso even more cuddles than normal. His blanket has fallen off his long body and I tuck him back in carefully. Helping him to stay warm and cosy. Helping him to end well

And then I pick up my iPad and start writing an email to Mum. Maybe I'll go and see her at the weekend. Probably I could play Pictionary with the boys. I could take Frog and we could teach them how to jitterbug. For some reason they seem to like me and that's OK, I suppose. Once I've done this I think I'll go out and join Dad in the garden. If I ask him nicely I'm sure he'll let us order pizza for tea tonight. It's been 191 Days With Dad and we're finally starting to figure each other out. Pizza helps. We can talk to each other over a pizza. Life is different now. Different, but still life.

This summer I've learnt stuff that I'd never have learnt at school – five things that will be so much more useful to me than fractions or spellings or stupid grammar. And I wasn't looking for any of it. This has been the best and the worst summer of my life. It has been the last summer and the first, and I will never, ever forget it.

Acknowledgements

It has taken quite a lot of people to create the book you're now holding in your hands and I am incredibly grateful to all of them for their time and support.

Thank you Adam, Zach, Georgia and Reuben who, as always, have been excited and positive about this whole writing adventure.

Thank you, Mum, for reading several drafts and helping point me in the right direction and, Polly, for your advice (particularly about Picasso and typical dog behavior . . .!).

My Aunty Helen, who lives in Canada, spent hours answering questions about her childhood and teenage years for me, as did my granny. Thank you both – some of your memories are included in this book and the rest are being kept safe for future use!

ACKNOWLEDGEMENTS

I also need to thank Erin B (whose name I borrowed!), Kate K, Amanda B, Paula L & Sophie E for providing critical feedback, guidance and encouragement in the early stages.

And thank you to Julia, Alex, Carolyn and the team at Puffin. I really appreciate all your support and hard work.